MEDICINE WHEEL

FIVE STAR WESTERN

MEDICINE WHEEL

A Western Story
by

Les Savage, Jr.

Five Star Western
Thorndike, Maine

Five Star Western
Published in conjunction with
Golden West Literary Agency.

August, 1996

First Edition

Five Star Standard Print Western Series.

The text of this edition is unabridged.

Set in 11 pt. Century Schoolbook by Minnie B. Raven.

Printed in the United States on permanent paper.

WES SAV
Savage, Les.
   Medicine wheel: : a
western story

Library of Congress Cataloging in Publication data

Savage, Les.
  Medicine wheel : a western story / by Les Savage, Jr.
  — 1st ed.
    p.   cm.
  ISBN 0-7862-0657-8 (hc)
  I. Title.
  PS3569.A826M43   1996
  813'.54—dc20   96-6301

Editor's Note

A condensed version of this Western novel previously appeared in *Lariat Story Magazine*. Certain scenes and characterizations, vital to the author's intentions and a reader's understanding of the actions of the characters in the story, were absent from this condensed version. Subsequently, when a book edition was published under the title THE WHITE SQUAW, this version had even more editorial omissions. For this first edition Five Star Western those scenes have been restored, based on the author's original typescript, so that now MEDICINE WHEEL appears for the first time with the title and in the form the author originally intended.

Foreword

by

Richard S. Wheeler

For roughly a century the settling of the American West has attracted the attention of many of this nation's best novelists. One obvious reason is that the Old West was colorful and romantic with its cowboys, longhorns, buffalo, mustangs, Indians, mining camps, honky-tonks, cattle drives, cavalry, and wagon trains.

But there has always been a deeper reason why the settling of the West has fascinated every sort of author from dime novelists to Pulitzer Prize winners. The Old West was the testing ground of character. It ate and destroyed weak people, including the reckless, while strong and principled men and women put roots down and prospered. The 19th Century frontier was dangerous. There were hostile Indians, justifiably angry about the incursions upon their lands. Starvation was never very distant because most staples had to be imported from the settled East. Law enforcement was either nonexistent or so thin that criminals could pillage unscathed, escaping down owlhoot trails into a vast trackless land.

In modern times a person of weak or malevolent character can often escape the consequences of his faulty behavior. Civilization permits a person to live an unpunished life regardless of his or her failings. That was not true on the frontier, where the consequences of one's actions or inactions were direct and stark. Storytellers have always understood that about the Old West and have employed it to create fiction of unusual power.

Such a Golconda of good story material did not escape the attention of a gifted American novelist, Les Savage, Jr. This author, whose career spans the middle years of this century, had the ability to cultivate any novelistic garden he chose. He had unusual command of the English language and was capable of lyrical passages about man and nature, but he chose the Western story, probably because more than any other realm of literature it permits the exploration of character. The perception that character is fate has been with us since antiquity, and it underlies our best drama and fiction. In this century it has formed the core of the Western story.

MEDICINE WHEEL is a powerful exploration of character and fate. With swift sure strokes Les Savage creates the entire story dilemma in the opening pages. His protagonist, Bob Hogarth, has arrived in Wyoming's Big Horn Basin with a small herd of cattle, the result of stubborn saving and scraping back in Texas. He'd learned from bitter experience and a broken romance that wage-earning ranch hands have no future. He is determined to do better, own his own ranch, become a person of substance — a person able to fulfill some of life's most important dreams such as marriage to a good woman. Along the way a collapse of the livestock markets has reduced the value of his herd to almost nothing.

In Wyoming he finds opportunity in the form of a ranching combine that cannot fulfill its contract to supply beef to the government for the Indian agencies. They need his beef but

8

can't pay his price; he needs land and security and the chance to grow. The deal is struck — more or less. Within the combine are various ranchers of varying strength and weakness, including a beautiful, red-headed woman, Kerry Arnold, daughter of a now deceased cattle king who once dominated the basin. There are also the Trygvessons, Viking father and sons, brutal, simple, and in their own fashion honorable. To complicate matters, we soon learn of rustling by someone on a barefoot pony.

Thus in the space of little more than a chapter the story is launched and the reader knows all the essentials. Hogarth has arrived in Wyoming with his sidekick, Waco, who understands Hogarth's ambitions and approves — so long as Hogarth retains his bedrock integrity. But Waco soon learns that Hogarth's ambitions override Hogarth's ethics, and from that point onward Waco is our conscience, and we readers begin to tell Hogarth to watch out: don't do that!

This Western story and its outcome hinge on Hogarth's character. He possesses the classic virtues: audacity that stops short of recklessness, determination and persistence, a will to achieve his objective of owning a ranch of his own, industry, intelligence, and a native shrewdness that keeps him from accepting land that lacks adequate water. In addition he has integrity. His word is good, and he commands the unstinting admiration of his sidekick, Waco, who came up the trail with him from Texas. These qualities — ambition and audacity restrained by a personal honor and trustworthiness — are the very qualities that in real life catapulted some settlers to the top, while other, weaker men faltered in an open land where anyone was free to go as far as his abilities would transport him. In Hogarth, Les Savage created a very real sort of frontiersman, instantly recognizable to anyone who has read frontier diaries and histories.

Yet, like most mortals, Bob Hogarth is not without tragic weaknesses. From the beginning of the story, he is taken with the lush, statuesque Kerry. Savage introduces her this way: "Kerry Arnold's lips were red and full, but their smile did not extend to her eyes. They were sea-green eyes, cool, watchful, sizing Hogarth up the way a man would judge a steer."

In two sentences Savage lets his readers know that Miss Arnold may be trouble. A few paragraphs later she draws her slicker tight, "suddenly outlining the lush curve of her hip," and a moment later she pouts. Savage pursues these images relentlessly, and the story explodes beyond the conventions of Western fiction, at least as it was written in the early 1950s. Kerry invites Bob Hogarth to her baronial ranch house and greets him in a dress of "silvery moiré, molded like paint to the upswelling arrogance of her breasts, the lyre flare of her hips." That evening Kerry frankly admits she uses sex as a weapon: "Her own arms were about his neck, cool, satiny, demanding. 'Don't be like that. What else does a woman have to fight with? When a man fights, he has his fists or a gun or a dozen other things. A woman has only this.' " They end up in bed, but not before Savage firmly draws the shade. Even so, it was too much for his publishers, and Savage's original manuscript, as it is presented here for the first time, had to be revised. The author had transgressed the boundaries of the early 1950s, writing sharply of desire, of a woman's sexual desire and a man's vulnerability.

SHANE, a great novel written contemporaneously with MEDICINE WHEEL, is far more circumspect. In it an attraction builds between Shane and Marion Starrett, but

10

Jack Schaefer dealt so cautiously with the triangle that the reader is barely aware of it until it explodes upon Shane, Marion, and Joe Starrett at the end of Chapter Ten. At no time did Schaefer permit the attraction to venture beyond the platonic, which kept the novel well within the public tastes of the day. But Savage was more daring, openly depicting desire and a woman's exploitation of male hunger in a genre that had heretofore been sexless.

MEDICINE WHEEL is a character-driven story. As fast as Savage creates a character, he lets that character play out his role according to his own nature and doesn't interfere for plot purposes. Unlike many Western authors, he slips into the minds of his characters now and then, permitting us to glimpse the calculation, the rage, the yearning, the underlying motivations of each. In the end he gives us vivid and memorable people, caught in the tense web of their conflicting desires. His gifts of characterization, along with an occasional lyrical passage, place him firmly in the ranks of the best Western novelists. Certainly one question driving the reader onward is whether Hogarth will ever perceive the trouble he's in or the nature of his own weakness — and what price Hogarth will have to pay in the end. I leave all that for you, the reader, to discover, saying only that Les Savage lets us know all along that there *will be* a price.

It takes a poet and true man of the West to write of the Western mountains like this: "There was an ageless indifference to the massive peaks, a sense of ancient secrets crouching forever at the backs of hidden glens and the bottoms of unknown cañons. It tugged at the wild things in a man, raised the hackles on the back of his neck, and started him looking for things he couldn't see and listening for things he couldn't hear." That is evocative language of the special sort that not only sings of nature but builds the underlying tension of the story. Les Savage, Jr., is an author any reader will enjoy, and it pleases me to present him here as one of the best.

Chapter One

It was raining the day Bob Hogarth and Waco Williams reached Big Horn Basin with their cattle. They had trailed the herd all the way up from Texas, and the animals were spooky and hard to handle under the downpour. Hogarth held them in a narrow valley outside of town while Waco rode in to find their customers. Hogarth circle-rode the steers on a skewbald horse so weary it stumbled every second step, while the rain beat on his yellow slicker like a tattoo of nervous fingers. He was taller than the average size, lean all the way down, with the quick and cat-like movements of a man who had lived much among animals and had taken on their nervous vitality. His blue eyes were filmed and red-rimmed from months without enough sleep; the stubborn shape of his square jaw was obscured by a three-month growth of sand-colored beard. He had been herding in the rain for two hours before Waco Williams returned.

"I think you got a deal if you want it, Bobby boy," he told Hogarth. "It's like they told us in Cheyenne. No big operators in this basin. Just this Big Horn Cooperative. Their main support comes from beef contracts with the Indian agencies up north. But the big freeze of 'Eighty-Seven hit them as hard as everybody else. They ain't got enough beef to meet their commitments. If they can't get some stock, they stand to lose the contract to an English firm that's imported some whitefaces for the deal."

Hogarth halted his skewbald before they reached a motte

of dripping poplars and turned to indicate the Big Horns, shaggy with spring timber, rising into a somber lead sky. "I bet this land's green when the rain stops, Waco. There's more grass here in one acre than you'll find in a hundred square miles around Devil's River. And the water. They say there's creeks up here bankful all year 'round. I think I like it."

Waco leaned toward him, a rare sobriety entering his voice. "Then maybe this is it, Bobby. If we play the cards right, maybe this is it."

Waco Williams was six feet three in his stocking feet with a sense of humor that spilled out of his twinkling blue eyes and kept him grinning like a Cheshire cat most of the time. His face wore a grin now, and Hogarth answered it and kicked his skewbald up the slushy slope, squealing and grunting, to where the four figures stood by their steaming horses in the shelter of the trees. One was a woman.

Hogarth got the impression of singular tallness for a woman, of red hair tucked beneath a flat-topped Mormon hat, of flesh the color of rich cream, whipped pink across the cheeks by the cold. Only Hogarth dismounted. Waco took off his soggy hat in deference to the woman. His hair was as yellow as his slicker.

"Kerry Arnold," he said. "Bob Hogarth."

Kerry Arnold's lips were red and full, but their smile did not extend to her eyes. They were sea-green eyes, cool, watchful, sizing Hogarth up the way a man would judge a steer.

"This is George Chapel, secretary-treasurer of the Big Horn Cooperative," Waco said.

There was not much to distinguish Chapel — average size, figure hidden by a slicker, flat-topped Stetson pulled down over careful gray eyes. Waco introduced the other two men

14

as Sigrod and Rane Trygvesson, obviously father and son. They were ponderous giants in thick plaid Mackinaws with something of the Viking to their long yellow hair, their glacial blue eyes. They neither offered their hands nor smiled.

Hogarth shoved his hat back on his sandy hair with the tip of a gloved thumb. "I'm going to tell you the story so you'll know just where I stand. I put five years' savings into these cattle back in Texas, and Waco and me drove them to Dallas. The day we got there, the crash hit. Beef dropped from twenty dollars a head to three dollars, no calves counted. I wasn't selling five years of my life that short. They told me the feeder market might still be holding up around Cheyenne. We got as far as Nebraska when the winter caught us."

"The worst winter in cattle history," Kerry Arnold murmured.

Hogarth nodded. "It wiped out half my cattle and nearly killed both Waco and me. When we got to Cheyenne, quotations were even lower than in Dallas. A speculator named Louis Moffet told me I could make a deal with you cooperative people. I've told you this so you'll know I'm not blowing hot air when I name my price. I didn't bring this beef through all that hell just to lose my shirt. I've got four hundred steers, and I want ten dollars a head."

"Ten dollars!" Sigrod Trygvesson's roar fairly shook the poplars. "That's seven dollars above the market in Cheyenne. You can't hold us up."

Hogarth's glance flickered to the huge Norseman. "You don't catch on very quick, do you, Trygvesson? I tried to make it clear just what these cattle mean to me. I'd turn 'em loose before I took three dollars a head."

The elder Trygvesson stared at him without answering.

15

Kerry Arnold moved toward Hogarth. Her movement drew the slicker tight, suddenly outlining the lush curve of her hip.

"Our contracts with the government certainly constitute a security as acceptable as cash."

"You're saying you don't have the cash?"

She lowered her head, looking at him from beneath the saffron sickles of her brows. Her lower lip puckered defiantly.

"No," she said.

He felt a rush of frustrated anger, checked it with difficulty.

He said: "If you're as substantial as I've heard, the bank would extend you enough credit for this herd."

His lean weight settled back onto his heels, and his eyes went blank. He had told them the history of this herd, but the brief, statistical account could in no way convey what it meant to him — the battles he had fought, the sweat and tears he had shed, the sacrifices he had made. It went far deeper than the actual struggle of bringing a bunch of beef through a thousand miles of dust and heat and stampede and storm and a winter so bad they still wondered how they got out alive. It went into the very core of him, bound up with the hopes and dreams of a lifetime. And that was why he couldn't yet sell those dreams out, even though he knew this was probably his last chance of salvaging anything.

Slowly he turned his head to look around at the hills, green as jade under the pearly mist of rain, with the peaks towering like smoke signals in the distance. He knew cattle land, and this was the best he had ever seen. It had been growing in his mind since they had left Cheyenne. When a man's string was played out, he had to take what he could get. But he still wasn't going to scrape the bottom of the barrel. In the long run the land might be worth as much to him as a good cash price. After all, what would he do if he sold the cattle? A part of his whole dream had been an outfit of his own someday.

"At ten dollars a head, I've got four thousand dollars' worth of beef here," he said. "Where I come from, land is selling at a dollar an acre. I'll deal on that basis, if you've got a strip that satisfies me."

Anger ran like scudding clouds across Sigrod Trygvesson's primitive Viking face. "We aren't letting anybody else move in, Hogarth. This cooperative was formed to keep the basin free of big operators and speculators like you. We don't want what is happening over in Johnson County. The land isn't for sale at any price."

George Chapel moistened his lips, glanced at Kerry, then said: "There must be some other way."

"Name it," Hogarth said.

He waited, studying their faces narrowly. Sigrod Trygvesson was breathing stertorously, clenching his fists, showing all the frustrated anger of a man more used to dealing with physical obstacles than with arguments — and rolling them out of the way. His son, Rane, was quieter, but there was a dangerous flush creeping up his oak-tree neck. The woman's anger was a thinner, more brittle thing, like a blade slipping from its sheath. Hogarth struck first.

"Half the operators around Cheyenne have gone under already, and any one of them could have bought and sold the bunch of you," he said flatly. "You won't have a cooperative if you don't pull through this year. And I have a hunch you won't pull through without my cattle. You wouldn't have come so quick if it had been any different. My terms still stand. I'll take land, but it will have to be good land, and I want an acre for every dollar."

17

Sigrod shook his head like an angry bull, his voice coming out in a frozen rumble. "No," he said stubbornly.

"Then I guess we're through talking," Hogarth said. He started to turn toward his horse.

"Wait a minute," Rane called.

"Rane!" bellowed his father.

But the man had already stepped out to catch Hogarth's shoulder. "You can't do this," he said thickly. "Williams gave us the idea a deal could be made. You know what kind of a position we're in, and you're taking advantage of it."

"Let me go, Trygvesson."

Rane pulled Hogarth back around, words coming out in a husky gust of anger. "You're right about us, Hogarth. We've had a terrible winter up here. It's pushed us against the wall. And we're not going to take this kind of treatment from a two-bit speculator who thinks he can shove us around." He jerked at Hogarth, his face twisted with his anger. "Williams gave us his word, and I don't like a man who goes back on his word. You Texas thralls think you can step in and play *fylke* king like a bunch of. . . ."

"Rane!" cried the woman, but already it was too late, already Hogarth had whirled around. He let his knee rise as he whirled. Rane's shout deafened Hogarth with animal pain.

Hogarth's shift to the side was as swift and calculated as his first turn had been. It placed him at Rane's side as the man doubled in spasmodic agony. It put the back of Rane's thick neck before him. Hogarth struck it in a vicious, chopping blow. Rane went face down on the ground.

"I guess not," said Waco Williams, and Hogarth turned to see the tall slouching man still sitting his dun with his saddle gun held casually across the pommel, holding them from whatever each had intended doing. Sigrod's hand was still on the butt of his Forty-Five. His whole body seemed held in trembling suspension by Waco's gun.

"You shouldn't have done that, Hogarth," he said in a choked, guttural voice. "He's my son. You shouldn't have done that."

"I think I should," said Hogarth flatly. "I think everybody had to be shown a little more clearly where I stand. Either a man puts his hands on me, or he doesn't. Either we make a deal, or we don't. I don't care to be handled."

"Sure thing," said Waco lazily. "Some folks are smart. They believe Bobby when he tells them. Others are sort of slow to get in the saddle. They have to be shown."

Kerry Arnold was looking at Hogarth closely. All the anger was gone from her face. That sea-green color had come back to her eyes as she watched him, and for a moment he thought a smile was going to rob her lips of their petulance.

"Very well, Mister Hogarth," she said. "Be in Meeteetse tomorrow at ten. The Bighorn Building. Oswald Karnes's office. We'll have decided by then what to do. We'll see that you're satisfied, one way or the other."

His own smile was lopsided. "Will you, Miss Arnold?"

Chapter Two

The spring rain stopped half an hour after they left. By that time Hogarth and Waco had set up camp under the timber. They kicked through the deadwood under a bank till they found some dry enough to start a fire. They rigged a rack of saplings over the flames to dry their clothes and boiled a pot of coffee. After three cups, bitter and black, Waco began putting on dry Levi's, singing to himself.

But one day he met a man a whole lot badder,
And now he's dead, and we're none the sadder. . . .

"Someday I'm going to find a 'poke that knows the rest of that song," Hogarth told him, "and I'm going to sit you down and make you learn the whole thing before I let you get up again."

"It's about Billy the Kid," Waco told him. He looked at his sodden shirt. "That slicker of yours ain't worth pinto beans when it comes to shedding water." He grimaced, slipping into the clammy garment. "It's too bad they have to be the slow type."

Hogarth took a last swallow of coffee. "Who?"

"Those Swedes. Those Trygvessons. The slow thinkers don't forget things like that. I wonder what Rane meant, calling you a thrall. What kind of talk is that?"

"Straight from the old country," Hogarth said. "I guess you'll find a lot of Swedes up through here. They stick together, take a long time to shed the old ways, probably even speak their own language at home."

Waco built a cigarette, squinting at Hogarth from his twinkling eyes. "So you're really going to do it."

Hogarth sat back on his heels. He looked down at his small, hard hands, covered with rope burns and calluses and scars.

"I've been trying to break in big for a long time, Waco. I guess you know how long. I'm through trying it with my hands. From now on it's going to be with my head. There's a chance here, and I'm playing it out to the end of the dally. Do you want to ride along?"

Waco let twin spires of gray smoke curl up past his saddle-colored face.

"I guess I know about that better'n anybody, Bobby. Some men were meant to take orders. Some weren't. Of all I ever knew, you were the last one I'd pick to do somebody else's dirty work. It always surprised me you stuck it out as long as you did."

"A man doesn't find out about himself soon enough, Waco. Maybe I thought I could make it that way."

"You got pretty far up."

"And came to a dead end. The only man bigger than the ramrod is the boss, and I'd never make that working for someone else."

"Soon or late I'm glad you found out, Bobby. It was eating your heart out. If it hadn't been for Elaine, I think you'd have cut free long before you did."

Hogarth was silent, staring into the snapping fire. Waco knew all about him and Elaine. The three of them had grown up together in the brush country of southern Texas. A hard, cruel land where most of the men were poverty-stricken shoestring ranchers, fighting tooth and nail for every rag on their backs and every meal in their bellies.

21

Elaine's father had been such a man, and it had put a fear of poverty in her that approached an obsession — an obsession Hogarth hadn't completely understood until it was almost too late.

He and Waco had come from the same barren background, forced out on their own while still young, signing up as cowhands on the Silver Bit, one of the few large ranches in the section. Waco had always been the footloose one, working when it pleased him, wandering off on some dim trail, drifting back sooner or later. Hogarth had been the steady one.

For Hogarth and Elaine had already found each other, and Elaine wanted a steady man. She wouldn't marry Hogarth till he had proved his steadiness, till he had built something that would stand securely between her and the poverty that had corroded her life. So he worked his way up from horse wrangler to fence rider, from fence rider to top hand, saving his money and waiting for Elaine to say yes.

There were times, as he worked, when he felt a restlessness in him. It was a different kind of restlessness from Waco's. It came from working for another man while there burned inside a fierce and basic need of independence, a want of achievement beyond the mere daily chores in another man's pasture. When this need became too strong to support, he talked to Elaine of striking out on his own. She had seen what that had done to her father, and her protests kept Hogarth at the grind.

The turning points of a man's life come in strange ways. When he had gone as far as he could along Elaine's trail, when he had jumped from top hand to foreman with an assumed future on the Silver Bit and had asked her for the last time to marry him, she had still said no.

Looking back, he couldn't blame her. Whether she had been deluding herself and had never really loved him, or whether she sincerely had wanted him, she was fighting something inside that was too big for her, something that had warped her needs till it ruined whatever chance of happiness she and Hogarth might have known.

He had been angry and bitter when he had at last broken his bonds, putting his lifetime's savings into these steers and driving them to Dallas with Waco. He had not left with the illusion of returning to her in triumph; she was probably already the wife of a man who could give her the measure of security she needed. Hogarth was angry and bitter no longer. He was surprised that there was not even much desire left to return and very little pain at the memory of Elaine. The one thing that did remain, burning more fiercely than ever, was his need to be his own man.

It made him realize that his loss of Elaine was only the culmination of something that had lain at the roots of him for years, making him chafe and rebel at taking another man's orders, at doing his dirty jobs, at making him rich. As a culmination that night had burned into him the bitter resolve that the next time he asked a girl to marry him, he would have more to offer than a saddle roll and seventy-five dollars a month.

Waco threw his saddle aboard and began to cinch up, talking around the cigarette in his mouth. "You told 'em we had four hundred steers."

"If we get land, we'll need stock," Hogarth said. "Last count was four fifty-three. Before I leave tomorrow morning, we'll cut out fifty of the best and drive them over into the next valley. It'll give us the start of a herd anyway."

"Right as Colonel Colt," Waco said.

He toed a stirrup but did not swing up. He was staring

23

across the back of his horse at the herd, barely visible in the gathering dusk. Finally he took the cigarette out of his mouth and spoke.

"There's something down there, Bobby."

Hogarth rose, staring at the distant herd. He finally made out shadowy movement. It was close to the toe of a ridge that extended into the valley. It could have been one of the larger steers.

Hogarth glanced at Waco then turned to heave his saddle on the picketed skewbald. The pony groaned and tried to blow up. Hogarth waited till it had to expel the breath and then jammed his foot against the spotted hide and jerked the latigo tight.

"You think it's them Swedes?" Waco asked.

"I don't know. They may want trouble." Hogarth slipped his bit in the skewbald's mouth, latched the brow band. "I'll circle around by the ridge. You go straight across. We'll get 'em between us."

He tossed the divided reins on the skewbald's neck and swung up. He turned the pony into the poplars and saw Waco wheel his dun animal toward the mouth of the box cañon into which they had put the herd. Hogarth followed timber as much as he could around the slope to keep under cover. He did not see again the movement among the cattle that he had first spotted, but the animals themselves were shifting nervously now, lowing softly, and the unrest was spreading. He made it around the box end, crossing the cliff edge through scrub oak, and went down the other ridge, careful not to silhouette himself against the sky.

The distance made the rider visible only by the difference of shape among the cattle. Hogarth gave a tug at the worn stock of his old Ward-Burton to loosen it in its saddle case beneath his left leg and turned the skewbald downhill.

24

Scrub juniper stood in warped rows on the lower slope, and he halted in this, trying to make out the rider more clearly. If it were Kerry Arnold and her bunch, there would be others. He searched the timber covering the slope on either side of him but failed to detect anything.

The bawling of the cattle had taken on a raucous irritation. If the rider intended a stampede, Hogarth could not stop him now. Yet, if the horsebacker were cutting out a bunch, Hogarth had never seen a clumsier job. It didn't line up with what Kerry Arnold would want. It drew a nervous anger through Hogarth. Finally the rider separated from the herd, driving one cow.

It was their old lead steer with the gotched horn. The rider was working the animal, slow and easy, up through the buffalo grass toward the junipers. The wily old steer was hard to drive when it didn't want to go, but now the rider was showing more skill. Hogarth was still not close enough to recognize the horsebacker. He began taking a line through the scrub timber to intercept him when he reached the fringe of the trees.

He could barely make out the pinto spots on the horse now. He had moved with great caution, keeping carefully covered. Any ordinary person would have seen him in this dusk. Yet, suddenly, the pinto's head jerked up, as if with a sudden pull on the reins. Then he heard it grunt, even at this distance with someone giving it the boot, and saw it bolt toward timber. This startled Gotch, and the steer ran into the trees right beside the pinto.

"All right," swore Hogarth and gave his skewbald a boot. It was a crazy race through the twisted trees. He could see the peerless horsemanship of the rider ahead, the pinto twisting and writhing through the close stands like a snake, sometimes seeming to double up on itself. His own horse

25

smashed into the junipers time after time as he forced it on through in a wild gallop, and he was dripping alligator bark. Gotch cut away from the rider ahead and ran bawling back into the valley. Then Hogarth saw the rider hit a trunk finally and literally bounce off, unhorsed. He couldn't help a cry of satisfaction and thumped his heels onto the skewbald anew.

The figure ahead had already rolled to his feet and jumped after the frightened pinto. He landed squarely in the saddle from a running leap over the pinto's rump, and Hogarth could not help feeling a thrill of admiration at such skill. The pinto wheeled up through the juniper and broke into an open glade and struck the ridge, silhouetted there for a moment. Hogarth forced his blowing pony up after it. He dismounted beneath the crest and went to his belly, worming his way to the ridge. From there he could see the next valley. This slope was not so heavily timbered, but at the bottom a line of thick cottonwoods marked a stream. He searched the area a long time, but no movement came to him, no sign. In disgust he went back to his horse and climbed up. He had reached the spot where the pinto had rammed the tree when a dim sound from below caused him to stiffen in his saddle.

"Waco," came the soft voice, and in a moment the tall, lazy man climbed his dun into view. "Heard a little ruckus up here. Miss Arnold's bunch?"

"I don't know."

Hogarth had dismounted and was staring at the juniper into which the pinto had run. There was a long red quill caught in the torn alligator bark.

"Just one rider on a pinto. And what a rider!"

He bent over the short wet grass, clearly showing the imprints where a body had struck and rolled, trampled by

26

the running feet. Finally he picked up something. Waco bent from the saddle to stare at it. The small cylindrical case was made of cherry wood and filled with a soft cottony substance that might have been swan's down, and in this lay the crude, feathered figure of a man.

"What in the name of Davy Crockett is that?" asked Waco.

Hogarth turned it over in his hand, and a puzzled frown tilted his lips at one side. "Could it be a *fylke* king?"

Chapter Three

Meeteetse was an Indian name for a place of rest, or far away, and it was the last outfitting point for the vast wilderness drained by the Graybull River. Sagging false-fronted buildings shouldered one or two newer pressed brick structures on Main, which was the only road worthy of being called a street. The Big Horn Building was a two-story frame structure on the corner of Main and First. Coming in from the south on the early side of ten o'clock, Bob Hogarth could not miss it.

He drew in his skewbald beside a sleek-looking roan bearing a Big Dipper brand. He gave himself time to scan the street while he took the rawhide reins over his pony's head and hitched them on the cottonwood rack. There were two men on the porch of the general store across the street. One leaned back on a rickety chair against the rotting boards, peeling an apple. The other lounged with one shoulder against the doorframe, thumbs hooked into a gun belt. He was a big man, thick muscled, broad shouldered, made even more impressive by the hulk of his plaid Mackinaw. He had the Viking face and the long blond hair, yet Hogarth was sure that it was neither Sigrod nor Rane Trygvesson.

Porch planks clattered beneath Hogarth's boots. There was a covered stairway leading up outside the building. Just before Hogarth reached this, a man appeared in a doorway down the walk, glanced at Hogarth's skewbald pony, then turned back inside.

There was a musty hall at the top of the stairs, a line of office doors. The first one said: **Oswald Karnes, Law Office.** Hogarth knocked and was answered by a woman's voice from within. When he opened the door, Kerry Arnold was rising from a tattered leather armchair by a widow. There was no slicker to hide her statuesque body this time. She wore basket-stamped half boots with spike heels that made her almost as tall as Hogarth. Her blue wool skirt was tight, clinging faithfully to the line of long, graceful legs; her silk blouse was tight too, emphasizing her mature breasts. It was a stunning sort of beauty that stopped a man in his tracks, completed by a mass of rust-red hair upswept on her head and the creamy texture of her flesh, turned to white satin in the dusky room.

She let him look a moment, without smiling, and then spoke.

"The others will be here in a few minutes. We held a meeting last night. I had to do a little persuading, but they finally realized it was the only thing we could do if we wanted to hold the cooperative together. Your four hundred steers added to what we have left will give us enough to keep that government contract."

He dipped his head in acknowledgment, taking in the rest of the room with a glance. There was a roll-top desk cluttered with papers, a swivel chair, a wire wastebasket. On one wall hung a pair of diplomas from some law school in the East, bearing the name of Oswald Karnes. Hogarth moved to the window. The big blond man was still standing in the door of the general store.

"Is that one of the Trygvessons?" he asked.

She moved beside him, the light tinting her curving cheek. A frown brought feathery lines to her smooth brow. "Those fools," she muttered. "I told them to stay away today. We don't want any more trouble."

"It isn't Rane."

"Sigrod Trygvesson has three sons," she told him. "That's Are, the youngest."

His glance dropped to the roan. "Your horse?"

"That's right. I'm the Big Dipper." She turned toward him, smiling wryly. "You should have kept your back to the wall when you entered."

He moved away, restless in this small room after so many months under the sky. "I just like to have things pinned down. What was that mumbo-jumbo Rane was talking yesterday? He called me a thrall, a *fylke* king."

She tossed her head impatiently. "Sigrod came from the old country. His sons were born here, but he's raised them in the old ways. He has what amounts to an obsession about it. You should see his house. Like walking into history. He rules it like an emperor. But there's really no harm to them. They're one of the rocks of the cooperative. It would have fallen apart more than once without their strength."

"And a thrall?"

She frowned irritably at his insistence. "A thrall, as I understand it, is a bondsman or a slave. A *fylke* king is a ruler of the petty dynasties they had in early times. The way Rane meant it for you, I guess you could afford to feel insulted."

"I don't suppose this would be his," he said. He took the small cherry-wood box from his pocket, showing her the feathery figure inside.

She shook her head. "Hardly. Looks Indian. Crow or Blackfoot. A fetish of some kind, a charm. I've seen them before. Didn't you have Indians in Texas?"

"I never saw anything like this," he said. Then he realized how closely she was watching him, with that speculative

30

half smile faintly curving her lips. It disturbed him and he moved back to the window, looking down at Are Trygvesson, still standing in the doorway across the street. "This cooperative," he said. "Isn't it something new in the cattle business?"

"It's been tried before," she said. "One of the biggest problems of the range has always been the fighting between the big men and the little men. It's ripping Johnson County apart right now. If it keeps up, they'll have a regular war over there. More than one operator has been ruined completely already. We wanted to keep the basin free of that trouble. It's one of the choicest sections in the state, and there are a dozen men on the outside that would give their right arms to control it."

"How do you keep them out?"

"We are each limited to three thousand acres of land. We can run as many cattle as we want but, as there is little free range left outside the basin, that automatically keeps us whittled down. We can make our own individual cattle deals, but all the big contracts are handled by the cooperative as a whole, and we share equally in them. That way none of us gets big enough to sway the balance of power in the basin. But the basin as a whole sees as big a profit as it would ordinarily. It's worked. The very fact that this winter didn't finish us for good is proof. You told us yourself how many men ten times our size had gone under around Cheyenne."

He ran the tip of his thumb across his teeth. "And if I accept this land in payment, I automatically belong to the cooperative?"

"You're hard, aren't you?" she said.

He turned in faint surprise to see her eyes were studying his small, callused hands on the sill.

"Hard and restless and grasping," she said, raising her glance to meet his. "Taught in the toughest school they have. Orphaned, maybe. Or ran away from home. Starting young, anyway, and learning the game the rough way. Enough brains not to be satisfied with punching cows or even hiring your gun out. Enough pride to want to rod your own corral. And now you've found something you want here, and you're moving in. How many times have you tried to move in before, Hogarth?"

His voice held a dim mockery. "How discerning of you."

"You're not difficult to read, Hogarth," she said, her eyes filled with that narrow speculation. "You're a type. A prime example of a type. I've seen others like you up off the trail. But none with such evident capacity. They were hard, too, but they didn't have the brains. I can't blame you for ambition, Hogarth, but when a man like you wants something, whoever gets in his way is going to be hurt." She paused to breathe, lowering her head slightly so that she was looking up at him from beneath the red arch of her brows. "You don't really think you can move in here like that, do you, Hogarth?"

He met her gaze without answering. She was clever. He had sensed it upon their first meeting, but now the impact of it was full enough for clear recognizance. A rare mind. A keen, pungent intelligence which would be more dangerous than all the Trygvessons' strength, if she chose to oppose him. He allowed a faint smile to cross his face.

"What do you think the chances are?" he asked.

"Under ordinary circumstances, you wouldn't have a chance. But you have us against the wall. We wired Moffet last night. He's our buyer in Cheyenne. He checked on you and wired back confirmation of your story. At least we know you're not working for one of the Johnson County operators

32

trying to get a toe hold here."

"Don't you ever get to feeling cramped?" he said. "When a deal comes along that would have made you big, don't you feel cheated?"

She was regarding him gravely with a strange look on her face. "I would advise you to keep any thoughts like that to yourself, Hogarth," she said. "It's one of the most dangerous things you could say in this basin."

He smiled thinly at her. "You didn't answer my question."

Her lids dropped, veiling her sea-green eyes. "They're coming upstairs now," she said.

Heavy boots were clattering on the hall stairs. George Chapel opened the door. He was in a conservative gray business suit, the pants cuffs filmed with street dust. He took off his gray hat in deference to Kerry as he entered. His precisely cut hair was the color of new hemp, parted exactly in the middle. He pursed his lips and dipped his hat slightly in greeting and introduced the man who followed him.

"Hogarth, this is Charles Tremaine, the president of the cooperative."

"Pleasure," said Tremaine.

He was a heavy-set, black-haired man with a black spade beard that bobbed as he spoke. His dark eyes were warm and expressive and his broad grin held a genuine greeting. Moving in behind Tremaine was a buckskinned Indian with braided hair and obsidian eyes. Chapel did not bother to introduce him. Behind the Indian was a man so fat he had trouble entering the door. His girth filled his white marseilles waistcoat in paunchy billows, a stiff white collar cutting deep into the doughy folds of fat rolled around his neck. His puffy cheeks had the unhealthy color of old paste.

"Oswald Karnes," Chapel said. "Bob Hogarth."

Karnes was panting from the climb. He fished a damp handkerchief from a pocket in his voluminous coat, mopping sweat off his brow. He lowered his chin into its myriad folds of flesh, peering at Hogarth from twinkling, pig-like eyes.

"Well," chuckled Karnes. "Bob Hogarth."

"If you'll get the maps, we can show Hogarth," Kerry Arnold said.

"Maps. Yes." Karnes waddled to the table and laid his briefcase on it. His little eyes slid around in a sidelong glance at Hogarth. Then he pulled out a sheet of paper and a folded contract form. The map was a strip of land just east of the Bighorn River, bounded by Medicine Wheel Creek and Big Stump Creek.

"We've marked off the south three thousand for you," the lawyer said. "Kerry told us you wanted four thousand, but she must have explained to you that any member of the cooperative is limited to three. We can't make any exceptions, Hogarth. Surely you'll be willing to compromise that much. This land has a south slope to protect you from the north wind we get here. Grass higher than your stirrups in spring. Watered by Medicine Wheel Creek the whole length of your southern boundary. You sign this transfer and contract and bill of sale for four hundred head of. . . ."

"Snub down," Hogarth said. "Change that strip to the east three thousand. I want water on both ends of my land."

Karnes popped his little eyes in surprise. "I thought you were a cattleman, Hogarth. You lose half your grassland on the eastern section. The upper end of the pasture would be all toplands with shale and talus."

"And Medicine Wheel goes dry in the summer," said Hogarth. "Big Stump is the water I want. Change it or it's no deal."

Charles Tremaine's gray eyes were wide and wondering. Only the woman seemed to feel no surprise.

"You didn't think we were dealing with a greenhorn, did you, gentlemen?" she asked. "Hogarth arose before dawn this morning and rode around the rim of the whole basin. I'll wager he knows every rock and every blade of grass like the palm of his hand."

Karnes moistened his lips. "How did you know?"

"Perhaps I understand Hogarth a little better than you," she said.

"So you had a man keeping watch on our camp," Hogarth said.

Her voice was ironic. "Is that against the rules?"

"Play any way you like," he told her.

Still smiling, she turned to Karnes. "Give him the east three thousand, Oswald."

Karnes shrugged, glanced at Chapel, pouted, looked toward Tremaine. Neither of them spoke. Karnes touched fat fingers to his fat lips, raised hairless pink brows at Kerry. Then with a chuckle that shook his paunch, he turned to the desk, swept a pile of papers away from a bottle of ink. Again he gave a quick little glance to the side, like a circumspect bird. The scratch of the pen was the only sound. Hogarth moved to the window. A second blond giant in a canvas-lined Mackinaw had joined Are Trygvesson in the doorway of the general store across the street.

"What is Sigrod's third son called?" Hogarth asked.

"Otherre," Kerry said. She came to look out the window, and her face tightened. Hogarth looked up and down the street. Then he turned back to look at the Indian.

"How long you had the Indian?" he asked Tremaine.

Tremaine pulled at his spade beard. "I'd say I've had Kasna five years. He was with me when I started the Big

35

Bit. An invaluable fellow."

"Maybe you lost something," Hogarth said, slipping the cherry-wood box from his pocket and tossing it to the Indian. Surprise caused Kasna to reach out and catch it. He stared at it a moment then raised his black eyes angrily to Hogarth.

"Lakota," he spat and threw it back to Hogarth.

"I guess it isn't his," said Tremaine. "Kasna's a Crow. The Lakotas are what the Sioux call themselves, I think."

"Do you?" said Hogarth. "This their pasture?"

"No. . . ." Tremaine seemed hesitant. "Not exactly."

"What's the matter?" Hogarth's voice held an edge.

Tremaine shook his head then said: "There's been a lot of unrest among the Indians lately, that's all. After the Custer massacre, General Miles chased Sitting Bull into Canada, you know. They caught him in 1881, however, and we thought the trouble with the Sioux was over. But Sitting Bull has started provoking trouble at the Standing Rock Agency. The Indians have been badly treated on the reservation, and there's talk of a new uprising. One of Sitting Bull's old chiefs has jumped the reservation with a lot of young hotheads. There's been a battle in the Big Horns. You're liable to find some Sioux down this way."

"A Crow wouldn't have the same kind of fetish a Sioux would?" said Hogarth.

"Definitely not," Tremaine told him. "What are you getting at?"

Hogarth was still by the window. He could see a rider on a prodigious white stallion riding in from the south now, just entering Main Street. Sunlight shone pale on his golden mane. Hogarth's lips drew back against his teeth.

"Someone was trying to cut cattle from our herd last night," he said.

36

Kerry Arnold tossed her head angrily. "Do you think we're that stupid?"

"You admit one of your men was watching us."

"A white man, not an Indian. And only watching. We couldn't unload your cattle on government contracts without a valid bill of sale, Hogarth. You're playing a hard game, and we're trying to match you. But we've got too much at stake here to rustle any cattle. We still constitute a legitimate business enterprise and will act accordingly."

The window was in two sections, the bottom half pulled open, and Hogarth tapped a knuckle against the dusty upper pane. "Is this the way a legitimate business enterprise acts?"

It was Kerry Arnold who reached the window beside him first, staring down to Sigrod Trygvesson, who sat that immense snowy stallion in the center of the rutted street now. "George," she said tightly, "they're coming in. The whole bunch of them."

George Chapel's boot heels made a small shuffle against the bare floor behind Hogarth. "There are some back stairs, Hogarth. You'd better. . . ."

"We haven't finished the business yet," said Hogarth. "Got that contract, Oswald?"

"Here's the pen, Hogarth," said the lawyer. "Right there on the bottom line."

Hogarth moved unhurriedly to sit on the edge of the desk, dangling one leg as he scanned the contract. They made nervous little shifting sounds about him. Karnes cleared his throat.

"This fifth clause," said Hogarth finally.

"The land belongs to the cooperative," said Karnes. "The clause is merely a formality to clarify that it is only the land we released."

37

"There's Rane," said Kerry from the window.

Hogarth reached for the pen and signed the contract and the bill of sale for four hundred cattle under the BH road brand. Each one in turn affixed his signature, George Chapel last.

"The back door, Hogarth," said Chapel again. "Wait in the timber behind town. We'll bring your horse when it's. . . ."

Chapel stopped as Hogarth walked to the hall door, opening it unhurriedly. Then he turned. "You have tried to convince me that you're not with Trygvesson in this. I'll believe you as long as you stay up here. If any of you follow me out, I'll consider him with Trygvesson, and deal with him accordingly."

He turned and went to the stairs, unbuttoning his canvas Mackinaw and hitching his gun farther around front. He halted a moment just inside the doorway, accustoming his eyes to the brighter outer light and placing the four men. Otherre and Are still stood on the porch across the street. On the opposite corner of First and Main, on this side of the street, Rane tilted one great shoulder against the two-by-four support of the wooden overhang projecting above the wooden sidewalk.

Hogarth stepped onto the sidewalk abruptly. The huge white stallion made a fiddling shift in the middle of Main with Sigrod's surprised jerk on the reins. Hogarth walked to the curb at one end of the cottonwood hitch rack where his skewbald and Kerry's roan were hitched.

"I've come for you, Hogarth," Sigrod said.

"How do you mean?" Hogarth asked.

The white stallion stamped his foot. "You know what I mean, Hogarth. Nobody handles a Trygvesson the way you handled Rane yesterday. Your man with the gun isn't with you today, and I've come for you."

The man tilting his chair against the wall in front of the general store let it fall forward, feet slapping the floor, and rose to step inside the door. That left only Are and Otherre on the porch. Hogarth sized them up with a quick glance. Are was obviously the youngest. His cheeks had been whipped pink as a girl's by the chill wind, and the beard on them was no more than a peach fuzz. Otherre, standing a little in front of him, looked to be the oldest of the three, perhaps thirty. His canvas-lined Mackinaw was unbuttoned, and Hogarth could see the barrel-keg bulk of his immense torso between the edges. Old rope burns made white tracks across the weathered backs of both hands, and the knuckles were swollen and scarred from some former breakage. It gave them a brutal look.

Hogarth spread his feet and shoved his Mackinaw back to put both hands in his pockets. "Sigrod," he said, "do you mean you've come to me personally, or are your three sons going to pile in alongside?"

The man straightened on his horse. "I told you. *I* have come."

Movement from Hogarth's side of the street caught his eye. Rane was moving across First, stepping up onto the sidewalk upon which Hogarth stood. There was something ponderous and inevitable about his advance. He had a slope-shouldered, flat-footed walk, rawboned hands swinging loosely at his sides. The boards popped and creaked with each step. Fifty feet from Hogarth he slowed down, eyes on his father. And Hogarth had the key to this now.

"What kind of sons have you raised," he asked, "that they can't fight their own battles? I hear you take great pride in your ancestors. Is this the way they did things? The Swedes can't be much of a race if they have to have the odds four to one."

39

Sigrod's face flushed deeply. "I told you, I. . . ."

"They can't even be much of a race if the fathers have to protect their sons as if they were daughters."

"Hogarth!" bellowed Sigrod. The blood was so thickly diffused in his cheeks now that they appeared purple. He was trembling visibly in the saddle.

"Maybe you've told your sons what to do for so long they can't even think for themselves any more."

At that Rane started to move faster. His father turned toward his second son, shouting his name. "Rane!"

Rane did not stop. He came on toward Hogarth, one big fist opening and closing by the butt of his gun. "I'll fight my own battles," he said.

Hogarth turned toward him, hands still in his pockets. "Every man should," he said. "But not without good reason. What's your reason, Rane?"

"Why do you keep asking? You know what it is. No man does that to me."

"And you'd call that a good reason? You'd risk your life, you'd take a chance on my killing you, just over what happened yesterday? That's a child's reason."

"No man. . . ."

"That's what your father said. Are you speaking for him?"

Rane's voice was guttural. "I speak for myself."

"Then do it. I don't think this is your reason at all. I think Sigrod has whipped you up to this. He's afraid to let a stranger in the cooperative. He'd rather see the cooperative fail this year than let me in. Isn't that the truth of it? Do you think that's intelligent reasoning? Would you do the same thing? I don't think you would. If you had the guts to think for yourself, you'd see the choice you had to make. Either take me in or lose the whole works here. And you'd take me in. You've let your father twist this all around.

You've let him make an excuse of what happened yesterday to whip you up, to bring you all in like a pack of dogs to set on a stranger. Aren't you old enough to decide why you want to fight, and when?"

"Hogarth!" Sigrod bellowed.

But Hogarth could see the indecision in Rane's eyes. The man had slowed again, frowning, and Hogarth pressed in.

"Rane, given a good reason I'll fight any man, anywhere, any time. But this isn't a good reason, and you know it. If you've still got to account to your father for every move you make, you'll come ahead and fight. But if you have the guts to stand on your own feet and make your own decision for once in your life, you'll forget it."

Rane took another step. Another. Then he stopped. The skin was stretched like a drumhead across his primitive cheekbones. His head was lowered, and his eyes were almost closed, and his mouth was like a scar across his face.

"Rane!" shouted Sigrod.

Hogarth saw a ripple run through Rane's body, but he did not move. While they were still divided, Hogarth walked out, unhitched his horse. Tossing the reins over the animal's head, he climbed on without haste. Turning the pony south, he passed Sigrod in the center of the street. He did not look up to the offices of the cooperative, but from the tail of his eye he caught a fleeting impression of Kerry Arnold's face in the window.

He went out of town, leaving the four Trygvessons behind him. Are and Otherre had come down off the porch onto the street. Sigrod had turned his horse about to stare after Hogarth in baffled rage. Rane was a confused, frustrated figure. Hogarth glanced down at his hands on the reins,

41

and one of his rare smiles spread his lips.

"What'd I tell you, Waco?" he chuckled to himself. "I'm through with the hands. From now on it's the head."

Chapter Four

The following day two men came out to take the cattle off of Hogarth's hands. Their names were Joe Hide and Morry Lucas. They both forked horses with the Big Dipper, Kerry Arnold's brand, and they had written authorization from George Chapel.

Hogarth waited until the men had driven the four hundred odd head out of sight down the valley, then he and Waco dropped into the next valley to get the fifty head they had driven there. Hogarth knew that sooner or later the cooperative would find out he still had some cattle, and he didn't care now if Kerry Arnold had a man watching, as she had before. It took them a day to drive the small herd across the broad basin and into the slopes holding Medicine Wheel Creek. After scattering them into the graze, Hogarth rode to a meadow crest and dismounted.

As he stood there, looking across the haze-shrouded billows of his land, feeling the soft black earth beneath his feet, something happened to him. He had always thought he knew what was driving him. The almost universal need for independence, for something of his own that lay in every man to a greater or lesser degree. He had seen it gnawing at enough others, pushing them, making them struggle and sweat and work their hearts out.

Now, standing here at the top of the meadow, looking across the emerald sweep of buffalo grass that welled out of the chocolate creek banks and rolled away into the shaggy jaws of the mountains, he realized that in reality his search

43

had been a blind and groping one. He had really only half seen what he was hunting, a vague and ill-defined will-o'-the-wisp that tantalized him, leading him on, always just out of reach. Even the revelation of his break-up with Elaine had not shredded the veil, had only cut him adrift for the first time to start the search in earnest. When he had made this deal with the cooperative, his plans had been vague. Maybe he'd stay, maybe he'd hold on a year and sell for a higher price.

But now the veil seemed to shred. Suddenly the dream was in his hands, fully formed, sharply etched, so fulfilling it almost hurt. This was what a man sought, and he could never know it till he stood on his own black earth, enveloped in the sweet smell of his own grass, feeling the touch of wine that would be blowing across his meadows for all the years to come. Hogarth knew certainly and surely what he was going to do now. He was through groping, through searching. This was where a man could stay. This was where he could stand or fall.

They made camp in the shelter of some timber, and over the last cup of coffee Hogarth told Waco what was on his mind. The man was glad to hear it. Then Hogarth told him how things might be worked out between them. Originally, Waco had signed on with the understanding that his wages would come from the sale of the cattle. But there would be no money forthcoming now, and Waco had gone through too much, had shown too much dogged loyalty, for Hogarth to continue regarding him as a hired hand. He offered a full partnership in the Rocker T with clear title to half the three thousand acres and half of whatever herds should accrue to them. Waco got to his feet, rubbing awkwardly at his saddle-brown face.

"I guess you know how much I appreciate that, Bobby,"

he said. His voice sounded husky. "But I ain't made for the responsibility of a deal like this partnership. It fits you like a glove. You got something of your own now, and you'll fight for it and work for it till the last saddle's sacked. But me, I wouldn't know what to do with so much land. I'd get plumb spooky, being tied down so tight. I just ain't made for a deal like that."

"Are you saying you're going to drift?"

Waco turned to him. "Not unless you want me to."

Hogarth laughed and got to his feet. He slapped Waco affectionately on the back. "I'd be lost without you. But you got to be something more than a thirty-and-found hand. How about foreman? I understand a good one draws down a hundred a month up here."

Waco grinned broadly. "At that rate, I'm makin' a hunnert a month more than you are, right now."

The next morning they rode into Meeteetse. They found that as members of the cooperative they had liberal credit with all the merchants. Hogarth made arrangements at Ab Kidder's general store to have twenty rolls of barbed wire and an assortment of tools wagoned back to their camp. They rode back with the wagons and helped the men unload. Their first need was going to be a house, and they started right in. They went into the timber and felled all day, straight-grained pine thirty feet tall. They scaled the bark off each log in a narrow strip, butt to tip, and snapped the chalk line down to guide the hewing. Hogarth hewed the first one and Waco mounted his dun and dragged the log at the end of a rope to the building site. When they had the hewn logs all dragged in, they laid their foundation stones and started raising the walls.

It was dawn to dusk work, leaving them little time or

energy to do more than sleep and labor. With the walls up, they made their shingles. They cut the logs into thirty-six-inch lengths, worked them into eight-sided blocks, then split off the shingles. It was noon of the fifth day, and they were lapping their clapboard shingles half on the pole rafter, when two riders came.

One was a man maybe five feet tall, almost as broad, with a frank and open countenance that had been burned by sun and whipped by the weather till it looked like a wrinkled beefsteak. He wore a tattered old Mackinaw and a pair of shotgun chaps, and his legs would have fitted fine around a five-bushel barrel.

"Shorthorse Simms is my handle," he told them. "This is Lee Dagget."

Dagget was a lean, slat-ribbed man with curly black hair and sharp slanting cheekbones that gave his face a foxy look. He wore a black bearskin coat that stank like the inside of a cave, and rawhide leggings that shone wetly with the grease daub of a thousand meals. He held his hairy little chopping horse on a tight bit, and it kept fiddling around and tossing its ugly hammer head. "Anybody got a quirly?" he said.

Waco got out his makings and handed them to the man. As Dagget started rolling himself a smoke, Simms grinned and said, "He's a chain smoker. Used up all my makings yesterday. I come from up Cody way. Winter so bad last year half the outfits went under. The rest had to give part of their crew the sack. Man gets pretty low on beans, a time like this. We'd be willing to work for our keep, till you started showing profit. I even got my own tools." He nodded at his big-rumped quarter horse. "Heeley here is only one of six, and all of 'em short horses. You won't get a better saddle string in the state."

46

Hogarth ran his thumb across his teeth in that absent-minded, speculative gesture. He could use help. There was a lot of fence to string, and there would be plenty of branding to do come calf time. He didn't like the idea of hiring grub-line riders, but in his present position he couldn't be too choosy.

He saw that Dagget did not wear a gun on his hip and raised his eyes to the man's coat. If he had an underarm harness, it didn't show. "How about your tools?" he asked.

Dagget saw where he was looking. He tossed Waco's makings back. Then, without smiling, he pulled his coat aside to reveal the Remington five-shot hanging in a sling under his arm.

"It stays warmer there," he said.

Simms was still grinning. "Dagget's worked the basin for a long time. Ask any of the cooperative people about him. Me, I worked for the Tincup, outside of Cody. You can check on us both at Meeteetse."

Hogarth grinned at them. "All right. Let's see what kind of fence you string."

They ate lunch, and then Hogarth rode out with the two men to show them where he wanted the postholes dug. It was late afternoon when he returned. Waco was still shingling.

"You don't take to Dagget," he said.

Hogarth shook his head. "I'm not sure. Times must be tight when a man will work without pay."

"I was down to the creek for water," Waco said. "Barefoot pony was in the bottoms. Looked like last night."

Hogarth glanced sharply at him. The words took him back to that day when they had first arrived in the basin, and the rider on the pinto had tried to cut out the steer with the gotched horn. He took the little cherry-wood case from his pocket, looking at the feathery little image of a man inside.

"The rider that dropped this had an unshod horse too, didn't he?"

"I thought of that," Waco said. He squinted at Hogarth. "What was the name of Tremaine's Indian?"

"Kasna. But he claimed this wasn't his."

"Would a white man ride a barefoot horse?"

"Hardly. But Tremaine mentioned that trouble at the Indian agencies up north would drive some Sioux down here, too."

Waco shook his head. "I don't like this, Bobby. There's something wrong in this basin. Those Trygvessons, so dead set against you. Somebody watching us all the time. Even that woman."

"What's wrong with her?"

"She's trouble. Can't you see it? Too beautiful. Too smart."

"Any woman's trouble."

"I don't mean like Elaine. I mean something under the surface. I don't like it."

Hogarth hardly heard. He was looking down toward the creek now, something working at him. "You say you went down for water. Were these unshod tracks in plain sight?"

"Couldn't miss 'em. They're right across the trail. When you bend down to dip the bucket full, they're right in front of you."

Hogarth kicked the bucket over, watched the water flow out onto the ground. "When Dagget gets back, let's send him for some water."

It was near dark when Dagget and Simms returned. Hogarth got the coffee pot and told Dagget they needed some water. The man lifted the bullhide bucket and went downslope willingly enough. He came back with a full

48

bucket, set it by the fire, went over to a rock, and sat down.

"Got a quirly?" he said.

Waco tossed the man his makings. Dagget rolled a smoke silently, staring into the fire. It shimmered greasily across the sharp ridge of his cheekbones and made a yellowish tinge at the corners of his eyes.

Simms was a talkative man and filled most of the dinnertime with harrowing tales of the hard winter. Dagget said little, sucking on his smoke, spitting now and then into the fire. Hogarth told them they'd nighthawk the cattle and gave Waco first watch. He went out with the man to where his dun horse was picketed, pointing out the sections he wanted Waco to patrol.

The lank Texan heaved his saddle aboard, muttering: "Dagget didn't say anything."

"Are you sure he saw those tracks?" Hogarth asked.

"He couldn't've missed 'em."

"That's why I want to keep a watch on the cattle."

Waco woke him at ten, and he took four hours. They finished the night out that way, four on and four off, without putting either of the other two men on a watch. If Simms and Dagget thought that strange, they did not speak. After breakfast they rode out to dig more postholes, and Waco and Hogarth went back to work on the house. By the end of the week the house was finished, and half the fence posts were up. No fresh, unshod tracks had shown up down by the creek, and the cattle had remained untouched. But Hogarth had not forgotten it, and something about Dagget still nagged his mind.

Saturday night Hogarth let Waco and the other two go into town, according to custom. He said he was tired and was going to turn in. He gave them a ten minute start then followed. He took a short cut down Medicine Wheel Creek to where the Meeteetse road crossed it on a wooden bridge. A bright moon was rising, so he stayed in the willows of the bottoms as they clattered across it. They were not talking.

He followed them for another hour to town. From the dark of a building at the end of Main Street, Hogarth watched the three men pull up to the rack before the Bullhorn Saloon, dismount, and go inside. Then Hogarth dismounted, pulled his horse off to the side of the road, eased the cinch, and built himself a cigarette. The shrill piping of crickets soon rose about him. Riders passed on the road and a rattling wagon.

Thirty minutes later Hogarth saw Dagget emerge alone and mount his black, turning it south out of town. Hogarth tugged his latigo tight again and swung on to follow. He stayed off the road, trailing the man through brushy sections and grassy meadowland. Finally the open range gave way to a snake fence along the road. At a gate Dagget turned down a wagon track leading through poplars to where the lights from a house peered through the trees. Hogarth let him reach the house, then followed. There was a sign nailed to one of the gateposts. **Tee Broom Ranch,** it said, **George A. Chapel**.

It was a tall hip-roofed Wyoming house with a stone porch extending the length of two wings. There was a spring buggy standing to one side of the steps, and Dagget's black stood at the hitch rack.

Hogarth thought the man had already entered, and he rode up quickly, dismounting. He was going up the flagstone steps when the voice came sharply from the blackness shrouding the porch.

"George?"

Hogarth recognized the voice, and it checked him on the

50

top step. In the same instant he said: "No, Dagget, it isn't George."

Dagget had no control over his response. It was completely involuntary, coming from violent surprise and from the thousand times he must have reacted the same way in the past. He had been on the point of opening the door and wheeled back even before Hogarth had finished speaking, his hand dipping beneath his bearskin coat.

Hogarth lunged across the darkened porch at the man. His right hand pinned Dagget's wrist against his chest just as the Remington came free. Dagget brought his knee up into Hogarth's crotch. It incapacitated Hogarth for a moment, allowing Dagget to tear his wrist free, whipping the gun at Hogarth's face. Sickened and enraged, Hogarth threw up his arm.

The barrel struck his forearm a stunning blow. With his other hand he caught the gun before Dagget could jerk it back and threw the weight of his body against the man. He pinned Dagget to the wall, and Hogarth tore the gun free of his grip with a violent curse, whipping it back across the man's face in the same motion. Dagget cried out sickly, and his body sagged heavily against Hogarth.

Hogarth stepped back and let the man fall. Dagget lay huddled on the floor, both hands held to his face, groaning dazedly. It had all happened in a few seconds, and Hogarth was still so sick from the knee to the groin that he thought he was going to vomit. That passed, however, and he heard voices and footfalls from inside. The door was opened, and light from within spilled in a yellow patch across Dagget, lying on the floor.

"There's your spy, Chapel," Hogarth said hoarsely. "Don't ever put one on me again. I won't stop with him next time."

George Chapel stood in the doorway in his gray business

51

suit, his face turning the color of putty as he stared down at Dagget. Then an outraged expression widened his gray eyes, and they swept up to Hogarth. His mouth was open to speak when someone's boots beat a running tattoo in the yard fronting the porch. A big rawboned man was running into the door's lane of light, a gun in his hand.

"Never mind, Templeton," Chapel said sharply.

The man slowed up, stopped. The extended wings of his old barrel-leg chaps settled in a leathery sigh about his long legs. He had an ugly horse face with bullet-gray eyes, and the sun had burned the ridges of his blunt cheekbones, his nose, and his brow till they looked red as raw meat.

"I thought you'd need some help," he said.

Kerry Arnold appeared in the doorway behind Chapel. "Seems to me it was Dagget who needed the help," she said. "And you're a little late for that."

Chapel glanced back at her, dropping his arm from the door handle to reveal the woman fully. Her red hair was pulled in a high coil on her queenly head. A sheath-like bodice of satin clung to her full breasts; a blue taffeta skirt whispered in rich folds from her slim waist. It was a sight that made Hogarth forget his pain. He felt a sudden throb of blood through his temples, and his mouth went dry.

She turned to Chapel. The tone of her voice could have been disgust. Or irony. "You disillusion me, George," she said, turning away.

Chapel's small mouth opened. He reached out a hand. "Kerry, I didn't. . . ."

"Don't make it worse," she said. "I'll get my own wrap."

He followed her back into the room, protesting, but she did not answer. Dagget had pulled himself to a sitting position against the wall, still dazed by the blow. He pawed his bandanna from his pocket and held it to the bloody

52

stripe across his face. Hogarth dropped the gun at his feet and turned to go down the steps. Templeton had not moved. He watched with a heavy-lidded indifference as Hogarth mounted his horse and turned it out into the night. His groin still hurt, and he was surprised that his mind was not on Dagget or Templeton. It was on Kerry Arnold and the first sight of her stunning beauty as she had stepped into the doorway. It made him remember Elaine, for a moment, and wonder why he had ever thought her beautiful.

He was half a mile north of the Tee Broom when he heard the rattle of a rig behind him. He pulled aside as the spring buggy came abreast with Kerry driving.

She studied his face for a moment in the bright moonlight. "Hitch your horse behind and step in," she said. At his hesitation she looked disgusted. "You don't think I was in on that?"

He did not answer, but he turned his horse to the rear and stepped off, hitching the reins to a brace. Then he climbed in beside her. She clucked her tongue and the spirited team of matched bays went into a high-stepping trot. She sent Hogarth a sidelong glance.

"Weren't you a little hard on Dagget?"

"I hadn't meant to touch him. He must have been real jumpy."

"I don't know what Chapel meant to find out, putting Dagget on you that way. But you must realize you've made us all jumpy. We had to let you in, but some of us haven't accepted you yet by any means."

"Like the Trygvessons."

She smiled ruefully. "You saw their weakness right away, didn't you? Setting it up so Sigrod couldn't put his hands on you without making his son look like a fool in front of the whole town. And Rane couldn't put his hands on you without appearing like a little boy who still had to run to Daddy for help." She had been smiling, but the smile faded. "That didn't end it, Hogarth. Sooner or later you'll have to meet them." She shivered a little. "It makes me feel cold."

He did not answer, and they rode on for a space with the moon-bathed countryside changing around them. They passed the town, and the dusty flats swelled into rolling meadowlands deep in grass. He was intensely conscious of Kerry's perfumed body next to his. He caught her watching him with speculation in her sea-green eyes, and he knew what she was wondering. *Why was he here, and what was he after?* But she did not ask.

In a little while they came to a fence zigzagging across the field like a snake. To his right Hogarth saw a double line of poplars leading to a rambling, two-story house. Its lower walls were of round stone and cement, its upperworks frame, its roof deeply hipped to shed the snows of this country. Studying it, he could see that there was not much paint left on the siding, and the shingles appeared warped and split. It had seen better days.

"The Big Dipper," Kerry said.

"That's sort of a castle for three thousand acres."

She pulled the horses to a stop beside the gate. There was a bleak look on her face. "When that was built, there were a million acres. My father was the first to settle this basin, Hogarth. He never knew exactly how many cattle he had, or how much land he used."

"The old story?"

She nodded, the bleakness becoming bitterness. "The old story. The fight between the big man and the little one. You know the old-time cattleman's empire was based on the premise of free graze. Dad owned a lot, but he grazed his cattle on ten times as much that didn't belong to him. Government land, open to anybody if all they wanted was water and grass. Then it was opened for filing."

"And the homesteaders came in. I saw it happen in Texas when I was a kid."

"Then you know how it ripped the country apart. The homesteaders got their toe hold. Control of water Dad needed, passage to good pasture, graze he had used. The Trygvessons are a good example. They homesteaded along the headwaters of Medicine Wheel Creek. When Dad contested their rights to water in the basin, they dammed up the creek and cut him off completely. That started the battle. If Dad had compromised, he might have been here today. Trygvesson approached us with the cooperative idea then."

"But your Dad was stubborn."

"He thought he'd have to sacrifice too much. He'd been the king, and he couldn't stand to lose it. I tried to show Dad it was the only way we could hope to last. We were at the end of the free-range era. We had to change with the times. But he was blind-stubborn. The war went on, the little men encroaching more and more, Dad fighting back . . . outfits burned, cattle run off, rustled, killed. And men killed."

She stopped, breathing more heavily, and he asked, "Your father?"

She nodded. "Nobody knows who did it. He was found on the range, shot. All I had left was the house and a few thousand head. But the little men had suffered, too. All of us would have gone under if we hadn't pulled together."

As she spoke, the softness had gone out of her face. Her lips had thinned, and the angles of her cheeks had assumed a taut shape. She was looking off into the night, and the moonlight made a silvery glitter against her eyes. It was a strange expression, not exactly bitterness or hatred, hard for him to define.

"Yet I have the impression you don't hate the little men," he said.

She sent him a sidelong glance then shrugged her shoulders. "It was an inevitable cycle. The little and the big were merely pawns. Johnson County is going through the same thing we did, right now. We've managed to keep it out by limiting the size a man can get to be in this basin. But this winter has presented a new problem. The cattle you brought us will keep the government contract another year. But we'll have to bleed our herds of even the brood stock to fill up the quota. There won't be anything left for next year."

"When will you get the government check?"

"April," she said.

Perhaps it was the expression on her face, or the way she had spoken. He sensed suddenly that it would not be her intellect he dealt with this evening. Maybe the night brought that out in a woman, or maybe the greater femininity of costume influenced her mood. He didn't know, but he sensed that her defenses were down. A faint smile curled his lip.

"What's amusing?" she said.

"Nothing particularly."

"I often stop here in the evening." Her voice was husky.

"With George?" he said and, when she raised her chin in that faint, defiant surprise, it put her in the correct position. Her ribs lifted against him with the sharp breath, and he felt the stiffening resistance in her body. His hard arm pulled her to him with a force she could not meet, and then his lips were on hers, and he felt the resistance leave her in a weak little wave.

He had known there would be this richness in her. He drank it in through her soft, moist lips with a thirst that surprised even him. When he finally drew his face away, she remained bent like a bow in her arms, her head thrown back, her eyes closed. She took a deep, shuddering breath, at last, and opened them.

"You really take what you want, don't you?" she said.

"I guess so, Kerry," he said. "The first time I laid eyes on this land up here, I realized I wanted it. All my trails, all my travels, I never saw range I wanted like this. And the first time I laid eyes on you, it was the same way. I won't say there haven't been other women. I won't even try to say you're different. Just more, Kerry, more than I ever dreamed could be. . . ."

His words trailed off as he kissed her again and, when that was over, she buried her face against his chest. "You're different, Hogarth, so different from these crude, shy, cowmen. Hogarth. . . ."

"Like Chapel?"

She shrugged. "He's the best of the lot. And he doesn't even know how to hold a girl's hand right. A woman needs something more than that, Hogarth, a woman needs. . . ."

"A woman needs the right man. That's all she needs. I knew it was right with us the first time I saw you, Kerry. Don't you know it, now?"

Her eyes were turned up to him, and it was the first time he had seen indecision in them. "As a man, yes, Hogarth. But this other, the way you came in here, your methods. Under other circumstances they wouldn't hold such a significance. Maybe I've been associated with the cooperative too long. You get close to people that way. We've been so successful, so free of the trouble and strife that has swept other sections of the state, with the constant battle between the big operators and the small."

"You take the attitude that my coming will change all that," he said.

"I'm not blind, Hogarth," she said. "Even in love."

"You don't seem to see what I'm after in a very clear light," he said.

"You've taken advantage of every situation you've met. . . ."

"Only to establish myself, beautiful. It took a certain amount of expedience to step in. Granted, I'm ambitious. I always have been. But it's not as destructive as all that. If I had a chance to step in on an open range, I would have ridden every horse I could to become the biggest operator there. If that isn't how things stack up on your closed pasture here, I'm willing to accept that. There are just as many ways of becoming big here within the cooperative profits, isn't that so?"

"Yes," she said. "But you aren't in the co. . . ."

"Don't play dumb, Kerry," he said. "You know what that fifth clause was. Karnes crossed a lot of pretty trails up in there, but I've been unraveling Indian sign since I was a kid. It comes down to the fact that, with my signature on that contract, I not only bought the land but joined the cooperative. How did you think that would block me?"

She shrugged, face still against his chest. "I don't know, Hogarth. None of us knew exactly what you planned to do. We could just see how fast you moved in, and there were so many possibilities. Even a rumor that you were an agent from the big Johnson County operators. They've tried to crack us before. As long as you're in the cooperative, your signature on that contract prevents you from having more than the three thousand acres allotted to the other members of the cooperative. Karnes thought that and the other legal restrictions involved would keep you from causing us trouble. Karnes didn't want to tell you till you made a false move. Then he planned to pop it."

"So you pulled a lot of legal shuffle to put me in a position I would have accepted anyway," he said. "And now I belong to the cooperative and, whatever I do, you profit by, Kerry. That's what I'm trying to show you."

She looked at him with a new calculation in her eyes. "Maybe you're right. Maybe we've coasted long enough up here. We've never had a really strong man, Hogarth. . . ."

"George Chapel's signature on that contract I signed was as secretary and treasurer of the association," he said. "Is he in love with you, Kerry?"

"I suppose so," she said.

"You've got enough cattle for this year's drive," he said. "But you've bled your outfits of even brood stock. What about next year?"

She shook her head. "I'm . . . I'm afraid to even think about it. There'll be a way. There must be."

"There's still some cattle down around Cheyenne," he said. "Some of the trail men were willing to accept the doubtful credit of bankrupt operators, but there were others like me who couldn't see it that way, and they haven't started back yet. A quick move could pick up several thousand head."

"We have no cash, Hogarth," she said emphatically. "Even when we get that government check, it wouldn't be enough for more than a thousand head at the present market."

"Time you get the government money, those cattle in Cheyenne will be gone," said Hogarth. "You wouldn't have to put up the whole amount. They're in such a position that they'd take half on speculation. Those trail herders wouldn't consider full credit, but five dollars a head down and a promissory for the rest from a reputable association like the

59

Basin Cooperative would swing it. Most of them in Cheyenne now are from Texas. I've got the connection. If I could send Waco down there with a check for five thousand. . . ."

"But we don't have any funds," she repeated almost angrily.

"Time that check is sent through and comes to the Cody National, you'll have the cash deposited from the government check," he said.

She tried to pull away from him. "Isn't that trail getting pretty shady, Hogarth?"

"Speculation, Kerry," he said. "You stand or fall by it now. You've got to. What's the use of hanging on if you don't have any cattle for next year, not even any brood stock?"

"And what if our trail herd doesn't reach the reservations? There are a dozen things that could happen. If the Indians are restless up there, it even makes it a greater chance."

"They won't bother their own beef," he said. "Of course it's a chance. But the bigger the chance, the bigger the rewards."

A flush crept up the milky line of her neck. She drew a little breath. "The others wouldn't see it?"

"They wouldn't have to," he said. "Only the man who signs the check for the association. And. . . ," he paused momentarily, that irony in the faint upward twist of his lips. "George is in love with you, isn't he?"

"Hogarth!" she said, stiffening, "what are you suggesting?"

Chapter Five

Neither Waco nor Shorthorse Simms was at the cabin when Hogarth returned. He rolled in and was asleep when they finally got back from town. He woke early and had breakfast ready by the time they rolled out. They both had hangovers and moped about camp like surly bears. Hogarth sent Simms to the creek for coffee water then told Waco about Dagget.

The lanky Texan sat on a log, holding his head in his hands. "You were right about him then. You suspicioned him all along." He squinted his eyes shut and stuck out his tongue. "Got a coat on it?"

"Like a grizzly pelt."

Waco grinned. "Forty rod they call it up here. Brings a man to his knees exactly forty rods away from where he drunk it."

"What do you think about Simms?"

Waco grimaced, running his tongue around the inside of his mouth. "I don't think he's in it with Dagget. I met a couple of grub-liners from up Cody way last night. What they told me of Shorthorse, he wouldn't be tied up in anything like that."

Simms came stomping back up the slope with the bucket. He set it down and spat disgustedly. "Tastes like I been chewing on brass, black powder and all." He put rope-scarred hands on broad hips and looked at Hogarth. "Some barefoot pony tracks down by the crick. Looks like it was there sometime last night."

Hogarth glanced at Waco, and they both grinned. Simms looked surprised.

"That's funny to you? I thought it might be an Injun making those tracks."

"There was some pony tracks some days back, too," Hogarth said. "We sent Dagget down for water. He didn't tell us about them. We began suspicioning him then. Last night we found out he was working for George Chapel."

"What?" Simms scowled at them until the implications reached him. Then he pulled up like a bantam. "If you think I'm tied up in something like that, you can take this damn' job and. . . ."

"Slack off, Shorthorse," Hogarth said, still grinning. "We aren't accusing you of anything. You told us about the tracks, didn't you? I figure you're a man to ride the river with. Fact is, I want you to stay here and keep track of the beef, while Waco and I look into those barefoot tracks."

That seemed to mollify Simms a little. They finished their breakfast, washed the tinware in sand, and saddled up. The ground was still soft from the rain and had recorded the imprints of an unshod horse faithfully. The rider had apparently milled around in the cover of the timber at the stream, watching the cabin, and had then turned eastward, going upstream. The tracks led directly to the herd where cattle had drifted into sheltered coulees and draws tucked between shoulders of the mountains. A rough count told them that no large number of their cattle had been run off, but the tracks ran right into a bed ground where a dozen head had spent the night. Simms finally got off his horse to take a closer look at the sign.

"Looks like he run off just one steer."

Hogarth glanced at Waco. "The same thing that rider on

62

the pinto was doing just after we first met Kerry Arnold and the others."

"It don't add up," Simms said.

"You stay here with the cattle," Hogarth told him. "Get a chance, string some of that bob wire. Waco and I want to take a look-see."

Hogarth heeled his skewbald onto a game trail that took him up into timber, and Waco followed. The tracks led them over the first foothill crest and on into the mountains. Soon the shaggy ridges were all about them, and the scent of pine needles was thick as syrup on the air. It was a somber country with bigger mountains than Hogarth had ever known in Texas.

There was an ageless indifference to the massive peaks, a sense of ancient secrets crouching forever at the backs of hidden glens and the bottoms of unknown cañons. It tugged at the wild things in a man, raised the hackles on the back of his neck, and started him looking for things he couldn't see and listening for things he couldn't hear. Waco kept glancing around, squinting at the sun, humming to himself.

But one day he met a man a whole lot badder,
And now he's dead, and we're none the sadder. . . .

Their horses were wheezing and groaning with the altitude, and the thin air made Hogarth dizzy. All through the forenoon the unshod tracks led them down brush-matted cañons, where beaver dams blocked every stream, and across saw-toothed ridges, where the wind whipped their hats till they rattled like drums. More than once Hogarth began to think this was greater trouble than it was probably worth. Then he fingered that little cherry-wood case in his pocket and knew he should go on. He was in no position to leave questions unanswered.

Sometime in the afternoon the husky cry of a saw-whet owl came from the dense timber on their flank. The unshod tracks led from bright sunlight into deep shade beneath a spruce.

"What do you make of that?" Hogarth asked.

Waco pulled his horse to a halt. "Sounds like he's honing a saw."

"They say timber Indians use bird sounds to signal each other," Hogarth said.

"Take it easy, Bobby," Waco told him. "I ain't ever seen you so nervous."

With an abrupt decision Hogarth moved his skewbald into a plodding walk again, leaning forward to balance his weight for the laboring little beast as it drove up the steep slope. Waco's rig creaked behind him. Hogarth halted again just beneath the ridge and stepped down to avoid skylighting himself before he saw what lay ahead.

"Hand me your dream book before you take a gander," Waco said, hooking one long leg around his saddle horn. "I'm plumb out of coffin-nail construction."

Hogarth's own tension stabbed him with a small, reasonless irritation at Waco's habitual unconcern. He fished for a pack of cigarette papers in the pocket of his Levi's and tossed them to the lanky man. Then he moved onto the crest. They weren't above timberline, and he took advantage of the stunted spruce, squatting down behind one to scan the slope dropping away from him into the valley beyond. Movement in the juniper down there was the first thing to catch his eye. . . . Then the rider came into view.

"Here's one," said Hogarth.

He heard Waco's big dun grunt heavily as the man swung off. Waco slipped the cigarette papers back into Hogarth's pocket as he squatted beside him. He scratched a match on a tree and put it to the fag he had built, cupping his hands and peering over them at the man below. Then he shook out the burning match and emitted a streamer of smoke with the words.

"Looks like Georgie Chapel is on a trail of his own."

The man was riding bent to one side, scanning the ground, and he came on up the slope that way. He was almost to the ridge when Hogarth rose. Chapel straightened with a jerk. One hand dipped toward the butt of a saddle gun, but the fingers stopped just above the dark oak stock. He let out a rueful little breath.

"I might have known it would be you."

"I don't fork a barefoot horse, George," Hogarth said.

A vertical furrow formed in the man's pale brow. His glance dropped to the ground again.

"How did you know it was unshod?" he asked.

"We saw the same tracks around our outfit. Took one of our steers."

"One? You got off lucky. About twenty of mine were cut out."

"This the first time?"

Chapel shook his head in bitter disgust. "It's been going on a long time. Always on an unshod horse. We suspected Kasna at first. But Tremaine swears it isn't him."

"How about these other Indians, down from the agencies?"

"If there are any around, we haven't seen them."

"Strange sort of rustling. Just one man all the time."

"If it's rustling," Chapel said darkly.

"What do you mean?"

Chapel did not answer. The anger still made grooves about his compressed lips, lent a pale shine to his gray eyes. Hogarth knew what he was thinking about. The man finally

65

spoke with distinct effort.

"Look here, Hogarth. About last night. . . ."

"I can forget it if you can."

"I'm not apologizing," the man said. "You play pretty close to the vest yourself. I think you might have done the same thing, if our positions were reversed. But there's something I want to know. Did Kerry . . . was it Kerry who. . . ?"

He seemed reluctant to continue, and Hogarth supplied it for him. "Who told me Dagget was your spy?"

The man leaned farther forward, his mouth a bitter scar. "She didn't . . . she wouldn't. . . !"

Hogarth smiled. "Remember, Chapel, I'm the newcomer."

The man straightened, staring at Hogarth. "Who then? Nobody else knew, but. . . ."

"But who, Chapel?"

"Oswald." The name left Chapel on a soft breath.

Hogarth did not answer. Chapel bent toward him, his words making a sharp hissing sound in the thin air.

"Tell me, Hogarth. Was it Oswald Karnes?"

Hogarth hesitated a moment then said: "What does it matter now? If I'm willing to forget it, you should be."

Chapel settled back in the saddle, staring fixedly at Hogarth. His cheeks looked pinched. His hands were cramped into fists. "That shyster," he said. "That two-faced, mealy-mouthed shyster."

Hogarth was aware of Waco, watching him intently, but he said nothing. Chapel was silent, looking beyond Hogarth now, lost in his anger. The wind sighing through the trees was the only sound. Then there was something else. The wrinkles about Hogarth's eyes deepened as he sought to identify it. He turned, frowning into the shadowy timber. He saw Chapel become aware of the sound, saw the man's fisted hands open slowly, saw the anger in his small face

66

grow to a puzzled frown. Waco was cocking his head like a curious hound. His voice was barely a whisper.

"Bobby, what is it?"

"Get the horses," Hogarth said.

Without waiting for Waco, he began to move toward the sound. It was still thin and unidentifiable, like the murmur of waters at a great distance. As he moved down the crest, followed by Chapel, it became more distinct, sounding now like the keening of a dog. Waco caught up with them, riding his dun, leading Hogarth's skewbald. Hogarth stepped aboard, and the three of them pushed through timber, keeping carefully to cover. Hogarth pulled his saddle gun out and held it across his pommel. He sensed that Waco had stopped behind him and looked back. The man's eyes were on the ground, and Hogarth glanced down. It was soft black soil here, bearing the imprints of unshod hoofs.

The tracks led towards the sound. They left the dense timber and came into a scattered stand of tamarack through which a definite trail ran. It dropped away from the ridge for a hundred yards then climbed toward it again. A ponderous bald peak rose to their left. Hogarth could hear the sound distinctly now. He halted his horse to listen, frowning as he stared up through the somber lanes of timber.

Chapel's voice sounded frightened as he whispered, "It's an Indian song. It sounds like some sort of Indian song."

Wanka tan han he ya u we lo
Wanka tan han he ya u we lo
Mita we cohan topa wan la
Ka nu we he ya u we lo. . . .

It came to them like that, rising and falling eerily, warped by the wind. Hogarth knew a resurgence of that nameless

67

tension he had felt before. The skewbald shifted nervously beneath him. Hogarth kicked his pony abruptly.

"Get in there while he's still singing, and the sound'll cover our noise," he grunted.

He drove his animal off the trail and up the steep slope toward the ridge above. But the singing had stopped. Now there were only the wheezing grunts of the horses and the rattle of shale underfoot. He came out on top and realized that he was clearly outlined there. He tried to pull back the horse back, but it was too late.

Magnified into an unearthly detonation by the thin air, a gunshot split the silence. The skewbald gave a startled scream and bolted. Hogarth's legs clumped at its barrel in the instinctive reaction of a man born to the saddle, and he even threw himself forward in an automatic effort to maintain his center of balance. It would have saved him but for a twist in the ridge. He was not yet fully recovered when the pony veered to follow that twist, and he was thrown off to the side.

He felt himself going and tried to kick free. There was a moment of uninhibited fall. Then his whole body jerked to a halt in mid-air. An instant later his head hit the ground and, through the dazed agony of that, he felt the whole weight of his body yanking at his foot and knew it was snagged in the stirrup. He had a moment of hope that the animal could not drag him very far up that steep slope. That was gone as he felt the speed accelerate, rocks and roots cutting into his back and bruising his head, and knew the animal had turned off the ridge onto the slope. It was so steep the pony immediately slid onto its haunches, squealing insanely. Hogarth kicked crazily at the stirrup, trying to tear free, his body twisted over and over as they gained speed down that slope, knowing any moment that the horse might roll onto him.

More shots came from above. Then Waco Williams loomed up beside Hogarth on his horse. The man must have put his dun off onto the slope at full gallop, and any moment it would go headlong. It took uncanny timing.

The dun came in beside the skewbald, and for that instant Hogarth was sliding down between the two horses, the dun still on its feet, the skewbald already in a sliding, rolling descent. With both hands free and knowing he would have only that moment to act before he too went out of the saddle on a rolling horse, Waco leaned down on the inside, grasping the stirrup on Hogarth's rig with one hand, Hogarth's foot with the other. Waco got in one tug at Hogarth's foot before the dun started losing its footing. Then all four hoofs went out from beneath the frenzied whinnying beast, and Waco threw himself off on the inside, still hanging onto that stirrup, giving another vicious tug at Hogarth's foot while he was in mid-air.

He came down on top of Hogarth, and the two of them crashed on down the slope. Hogarth heard his own gasp of pain. He was so dazed by the dragging now that he didn't realize his foot was free of the stirrup till they rolled to a stop against a boulder. Both horses went sliding on down the hill, crashing past a stunted juniper, an avalanche of rocks and shale accompanying them.

Hogarth heard himself groaning. It sounded far away. After hearing came feeling. Pain split his skull. There was a wrenched agony in his right leg.

"You all right, Bobby?"

Hogarth nodded and rose to one elbow. Waco sprawled beside him across the brown moss on the boulder. There was a broad grin on his bleeding face. Hogarth glanced down the steep slide to where the skewbald had finally stopped by a warped mat of junipers. Its body lay broken and twisted and motionless, the way Hogarth would have been if Waco had not pulled his foot free. The dun was not in sight and must have gone on down the slide into the timber far below. Hogarth looked back up at the edge of the trail so far above where Waco had deliberately driven the dun over after him. Finally Hogarth looked at Waco.

"Thanks," he said simply.

"Done the same thing a million times bulldoggin' a steer," Waco said. "That's all it took."

"I know what it took," Hogarth told him. He sucked in a breath, looking at the trail again. "Chapel's out of sight. I thought it was funny, him coming along like that. He doesn't seem like the type."

"You said he had a man named Templeton."

"And one named Dagget," Hogarth said.

"What about the Indian we heard singing?"

"How do we know it was an Indian?"

"Didn't sound like no white man to me."

Hogarth was silent, studying the slide ahead. Finally he said: "That trail drops down level with us farther along. No use fighting this slide back up. We'll be exposed that way. Let's work across the slope through that scrub timber."

They started moving through the rocks and twisted junipers, keeping themselves covered from above as well as possible. Hogarth had to drag his leg. After a few hundred feet he had to stop in a mat of brush, panting, dizzy. Waco crouched beside Hogarth, studying him.

"How come you wanted Chapel to think it was Oswald Karnes that told you about Dagget?" he asked.

"It was Chapel's own idea."

"But you didn't deny it. He thought it was Karnes, and you let him go on thinking it."

70

Hogarth felt a dim apprehension touch him, and his head raised. "Divided we fall, Waco."

"That might work both ways, Bobby," said Waco.

"How do you figure?"

"I always opined a ranny capable of crossing one man was capable of crossing any man," said Waco.

"Not crossing them," said Hogarth. "There just has to be a wedge to use. If Chapel has a temper, and we can use it as a wedge between him and Karnes. . . ." He stopped, only then realizing the full implications of what Waco had said. He stared at the man. Finally he said: "You don't really think that, Waco, do you?"

"I never thought of it before in connection with you and me, Bobby," said Waco. "I been with you now long enough to know how sharp your edge is. But no matter how quick you changed leads in the past, you always kept your hoofs clean. You never gave me cause to ask myself a question like that."

"But what possible reason could I have for. . . ?"

"Who knows?" said Waco. "One might come along."

"When men get to talking like this, Waco," said Hogarth, meeting his eyes, "it's time to end the roundup."

"Let's pull up stakes," said Waco with an impulsiveness foreign to him, clutching Hogarth's arm. "Let's saddle up and hit the trail, Bobby. This isn't good pasture. The grass looks greener, but it's rotten. It'll kill the stock, Bobby. . . ."

Hogarth shook his head. "You know how long I've been trying for a spot like this. We're in now, Waco. I'm not throwing aces like this away."

Waco regarded him silently for a moment, shrugged heavily. "All right, Bobby. We'd better shift here then. That rifle is still around somewhere."

Hogarth started crawling to the next cover, and it wasn't

his leg dragging him down now. He had a strange empty feeling at the pit of his stomach.

The trail reached its peak and then started dropping down toward them. They rounded a shoulder of the slope to see that it passed them, going on down into a broad meadow. Hogarth crawled into a motte of stunted spruce, staring at what lay in the meadow. That same tension he had felt before started forming once more. Waco crawled in beside him, and his mouth opened slightly as he saw what Hogarth was looking at.

"What is it?" he whispered.

Hogarth shook his head, not able to answer. In the meadow below them was a gigantic wheel of limestone slabs and boulders fully a hundred feet across. The hub was a circular mound, worn smooth and gleaming either by human fashioning or ages of weathering. From this radiated spokes made up of the slabs. At the end of some of the spokes were what looked like shelters built of stone. On the top of one of these shelters was a bleached buffalo skull. Hogarth could not understand that ineffable awe it produced in him.

"Remember Pecos?" said Waco.

"This doesn't look like any pueblo ruin," said Hogarth. "Make you feel funny?"

Waco nodded vaguely. "Looks like someone built a fire in front of that building with the buffalo skull on top. Maybe where the singing was coming from?"

Hogarth felt his body go rigid. A man had appeared suddenly from behind one of the stone buildings on the far side, near the lower end of the slightly sloping meadow. He carried a rifle in one hand and was bent over the ground. He moved on through the limestone slabs.

"Cover me," said Hogarth and started down through the

spruce, forgetting in action what had gone between him and Waco a few minutes before. He moved with the swift, efficient capacity that came with utter confidence in Waco's ability to back him to the hilt, a confidence born of the peerless, unified teamwork they had developed.

He forgot the pain of his leg in the restrained excitement of stalking the man below. He found a spot where the trees almost reached one end of a spoke in the giant wheel and flitted from them in a soundless limping run, reaching the first limestone block to crouch there a moment, controlling his breathing carefully to listen. Finally he caught the faint crunch of a footstep.

He dodged up the line of slabs till he was about half way to the hub, halting again. From this position he could hear the passage of the man more clearly. Evidently he was crossing between the spokes, moving in his direction. The wooden butt of Hogarth's Forehand & Wadsworth was smooth and comforting in his hand. He hooked his thumb around the big single-action hammer. His head lifted.

The limestone slabs forming the spokes were laid a few feet apart, and through one of these openings the man had come, three blocks down from Hogarth. He walked in a smooth, catty way with an old carbine tucked in one elbow. Hogarth allowed him to get far enough out in the open.

"All right," he said. "Just stop and drop the carbine before you turn around."

The normal man would have stiffened, probably, in surprise. This one didn't. He stopped with no appreciable change in the feline expression of his body. Then he lowered the Spencer carefully to the ground and turned around.

From the back Hogarth had not recognized the man. Now he saw that he was Charles Tremaine's Indian, Kasna. Hogarth met his obsidian eyes for a moment then asked:

"Was that you singing?"

The man's face was as enigmatic as wood. "No," he said.

"What are you doing here?"

"Same as you, maybe. I hear song. I come look."

Waco must have seen what had happened from upslope, for the crunch of his boots in the deep layer of pine needles reached Hogarth. In a moment he appeared, rounding the end of one of the spokes in the great wheel. He stopped, staring blankly at Kasna.

"What'd I tell you?" he said. "It gets uglier all the time."

Chapter Six

No amount of questioning would make Kasna tell why he was there. But he finally agreed to see if Waco's horse was still alive. In an hour he came back with the animal. He said Hogarth's skewbald was dead at the bottom of the slide, but he had found the dun grazing a mile away. The blood of a dozen surface wounds was clotted on its hide, and it limped heavily, but none of its legs seemed broken. If they rode at a walk, it could carry them double without much trouble. They left Kasna and did not get back to the Rocker T till long after midnight. They passed through a section of barbed wire that Simms had strung and found the man circle-riding the cattle. He said nothing had happened, and Hogarth relieved him, sending the two men to the house while he took a watch on the herd. He knew they couldn't keep this up all the time, but he was reluctant to let the cattle drift till they found out about those barefoot pony tracks.

Near dawn Waco relieved him, and Hogarth rolled in to sleep until noon. He left them to work on the fence then and rode into Meeteetse. The barman in the Bullhorn was named Jigger, a bald-headed Irishman with cauliflower ears, twinkling blue eyes, and a barroom scar across one cheek. Hogarth had a beer and asked the man if Chapel had been in yet. Jigger told him not today, and Hogarth walked over to look out the front window.

Through the dusty glass he could see the Big Horn Building across the street in which Oswald Karnes had his office.

This was something Hogarth didn't care for, any more than Waco. But he had been given a wedge by Chapel's suspicion. He suspected what was in Chapel's mind concerning Karnes and meant to use their clash for what it was worth. Hogarth let his glance wander north on Main, passing the harness shop next to the Big Horn Building, the false-fronted Fetterman Hotel, the big red barn of Gilroy's stable on the corner of Second and Main.

The group of idlers before the stable stirred, staring toward the man who opened the door and came down the side stairs of the hotel. The stairs led to Doc Powdre's office on the second floor, but the man was not Powdre. He was dressed in a black bearskin coat and the whole left side of his face was plastered up with a white bandage. He moved in a quick foxy walk to the rack, knocked the reins of his horse loose, swung them over the animal's head, stepped aboard, and headed out of town. Hogarth returned to the bar.

Jigger had been watching also and now and leaned toward Hogarth. "Dagget has come in every day for that face of his. Doc says he'll have the scar for life."

"Maybe he won't be so quick to pull his gun on a man next time," Hogarth observed.

"Or maybe quicker," Jigger said. "If it's the right man."

Hogarth glanced at the bartender. Jigger's face was blank. Hogarth asked: "What did you do to the man who gave you that scar?"

Jigger touched his cheek, grinning. "I bought him a beer. The quickest way to an Irishman's heart is to fight him."

Hogarth smiled thinly and sipped at his beer. One of the group before the stables had detached himself and came unhurriedly down the street. It was Charles Tremaine, the black-bearded president of the Big Horn Cooperative, big, hearty, and genial in his red wool shirt and new Levi's held

76

up by a pair of snakeskin galluses.

It struck Hogarth that a man could learn a lot about a town just by watching the pattern of movement through its streets. Tremaine saw the doctor come out on his balcony and waved a hand at him, grinning broadly. Then he turned to Ab Kidder, who sat tilted in his chair on the porch of the general store, and passed some joking comment to him as he went by. Kidder stopped paring his apple and answered with a smile.

"Tremaine's well liked in town," Hogarth said.

"Hasn't got a single enemy," Jigger observed.

The black-bearded man entered the saloon, greeted Jigger, then saw Hogarth. He walked over, snapping his galluses, and smiled broadly.

"Didn't see your skewbald outside," he said.

"I'm forking that short horse at the rack," Hogarth said. "Lost my skewbald in a slide yesterday, up in the mountains. Didn't Kasna tell you?"

"He told me he saw you up there. He didn't say anything about the horse."

Hogarth saw no guile in the man's broad and swarthy face and invited him to sit and have a beer. After being served, Tremaine led the way over to a table. Once they were settled, Hogarth said: "Kasna wouldn't say what he was doing at that pile of stones."

"It has religious significance to a lot of the Indians around here, Hogarth. They call the place Medicine Wheel. But they don't really know what it is. They have no legends or traditions to explain its origin. It must have belonged to a prehistoric race. The pattern and orientation imply sun worship. There was a professor up here last year who tried to connect it with the Aztecs. There are twenty-nine spokes, possibly representing the days of the lunar month. Those six buildings around the edge of the wheel are called medicine teepees by the Crows. It has always fascinated me. Sort of gives you the creeps."

"You really know your Indians," Hogarth said. "Maybe you can tell me what we heard up there."

"The song, you mean? Kasna heard it, too. He said it was the Sioux Song of the Sun. I've heard it at their sundance ceremonies."

"Would that bring us back to some of those Sioux, down from the agencies in this uprising?"

"Perhaps," Tremaine said. "You haven't told me why you were up there."

Hogarth realized there would be no point in hiding it, since Chapel already knew. He watched carefully for reaction in the man's face as he spoke. "We were on the trail of an unshod horse, Tremaine." Hogarth saw the flutter of muscle run across Tremaine's jaw and bent toward him, asking: "Have they been working on you too?"

Tremaine nodded. "On all of us, Hogarth. That unshod horse made them suspect Kasna. But I'm sure it isn't him. I can't even believe it's other Indians. They would do it only for meat. A dozen steers at a time would indicate a group of forty or fifty Sioux. That many down here in one bunch would have a whole regiment of troops after them."

"They only took one steer from my herd," Hogarth said.

Tremaine's eyes widened in surprise. Then he shook his head, gazing blankly at Hogarth. "That's a new twist. One steer. It doesn't make sense. It's always been twenty or thirty from my herd. We've tried every method of stopping it. Kasna and I have nighthawked the herd for a month straight. But none of our outfits is big enough for a night-and-day watch indefinitely. And as soon as we quit, the rider hits again. Kasna has tried to follow the tracks a dozen

78

times. But even he can't get much beyond Medicine Wheel. It's really badlands east of there. Nothing but sand and shale and rock slides, for miles. Hard rock might take scars, at least, but that sliding stuff is hell for a tracker to get any sign out of."

"Isn't the Hole-in-the-Wall country over there somewhere?"

"Way over," Tremaine said. "I've thought of that, too. Hole-in-the-Wall is as much legend as fact. They'd have you believe every long rider from Sam Bass to Billy the Kid is hiding in there."

"A logical place to take the cattle."

Tremaine shook his head. "The only known entrance is on the eastern side of the mountains, over by the Powder. It would be impossible for this rider on the barefoot horse to keep trailing the cattle that far without being discovered by someone sooner or later."

"How about a way in from this side?"

"There have been stories about a western entrance, ever since I was a kid. But I've lived here all my life, Hogarth, and never met anybody who had seen it. My father was a fur trapper for Hudson's Bay and knew the country as well as the Indians. Even he didn't know of any western entrance. He did tell me once that this Indian, Yellow Elk, claimed to know the way in. But it had something to do with a white buffalo and Medicine Wheel. It's impossible to separate fact from fancy when those Indians get mixed up with their religion." Tremaine shook his head again. "The whole thing isn't logical anyway. Did you ever hear of a rustler hanging onto the stuff he took? The only reason he takes it is for quick money."

"We keep talking of an Indian on that barefoot horse. Could it be a white man, riding an unshod pony to throw

79

suspicion on the Indians?"

Something fluttered through Tremaine's eyes. He looked at Hogarth, dropped his gaze to the floor. He twirled the glass. "I doubt it," he said.

A pair of horsemen had appeared on the road, coming from the south. With his eyes following them in, Hogarth said: "Kerry told me that when her father was the king here, the Trygvessons did all they could to pull him down. Did that include rustling his stock?"

Tremaine's chin lifted sharply, eyes dancing brightly. "What are you driving at?"

One of the horses was a claybank with George Chapel in the saddle. Hogarth watched the man pull it in to the hitch rack in front of the Big Horn Building with the second man following him in. It was Templeton, tall and horsefaced with the raw sunburn on the bony ridges of his blunt cheekbones and his lantern jaw.

Hogarth took his eyes from them to smile thinly at Tremaine. "I've made you mad. I didn't think it could happen. I must have touched a tender spot, Tremaine. Could it be that each one of you in this cooperative suspects one of the other members of this rustling?"

Tremaine leaned across the table, speaking tensely. "Listen, Hogarth. I've tried to treat you decently. The others are suspicious of you, but I believe in giving every man a fair chance. I've been a part of Meeteetse since it was Yellow Elk's Indian camp, and I haven't made an enemy yet. Don't make me start this late in life. Every one of these people in the cooperative is an old friend of mine. They have their faults, but they're not rustlers."

Chapel and Templeton had dismounted now and were going upstairs in the Big Horn Building. Hogarth stood up. He had the feeling that Tremaine's offer of friendship was

80

sincere, and he wanted to accept it. "I'm sorry, Tremaine," he said. "I appreciate the way you've treated me. I want to belong here. I'll forget what I said if you will."

Tremaine leaned back, scowling. Then he lifted his broad shoulders, dropped them. "I'll forget."

"Good." Hogarth put a hand on his shoulder. "Come up soon and see what we're doing with that Medicine Wheel land. I think you'll like it."

Tremaine nodded, and Hogarth went out the door, dragging his bad leg. The quarter horse Simms had loaned him was at the rack, and he gave it a pat on its rump as he passed. He crossed the street and went around the claybank and the other horse with the Tee Broom brand. He walked carefully up the stairs. They creaked a couple of times near the top. The door of Oswald Karnes's law office was ajar, and the voices came clearly through that.

"You planted Lee Dagget on Hogarth?" It was Karnes's voice, high and nasal. "How did you manage that, George?"

"Don't try to cover up, Oswald," Chapel said spitefully. "How did you know? Do you have strings on Dagget, too?"

"Strings on Dagget? I haven't talked with the man in a month. I haven't even seen Hogarth since the first day."

"Can you prove it, Oswald?"

"Prove it?"

"You're a lawyer, Oswald. Where's your alibi?"

"Alibi?"

"Where were you night before last about six, Oswald? You weren't here. You weren't at home. Can you prove you weren't seeing Hogarth?"

"George, I . . . I. . . ."

"So you were seeing him." There was a sharp scrape of boots. "I'm fed up with you, Oswald. Ever since you first started handling our legal business, you've surrounded your

81

actions with such a veil of legal terminology and verbal double shuffle that none of us knows where we stand. I'm sick of it. I'm bringing up a motion the next time the board meets to have you removed as our attorney."

"Removed? Chapel, you have no excuse. How could I have known your connection with Lee Dagget? Don't be a fool about this. Can't you see what that kind of motion would do to us now? We're already in hot water. Those cattle of Hogarth's will pull us out only momentarily. What about next year? We haven't even got any brood stock left. With quotations rising again, that government check won't be enough to restock our ranges when it does come. We've got to stick together more than ever. We've got to find some way out of this."

"You can't smoke up the issue this time, Oswald. I guess you know what happened to Dagget. Hogarth thought it would be a warning to me. I'm going to show him two can ride that horse. I'm going to do to his man exactly what he did to mine, so when he sees you, he'll know."

"George, no!"

"Hold him, Templeton."

"George, no, please, no Chapel. . . !"

"Yes, Oswald."

"No, George," Hogarth said.

He spoke as he stepped into the room. His voice stopped all three of them for an instant. Oswald Karnes was backed up against the desk with both plump hands held up in the air, his little mouth open. Templeton had grabbed one of his wrists, fingers digging deep into the puffy flesh. Chapel stood with his back to Hogarth, hand on his gun. He must have thought Hogarth had him covered, for he did not turn. But Templeton could see Hogarth and said sharply: "His iron isn't skinned."

Chapel reacted instantly to the words, wheeling and drawing at the same time. Hogarth lunged against the man. His down-swinging fist knocked the six-shooter from Chapel's hand as it cleared the holster. He let his rush carry him heavily against the man, knocking Chapel backward and off his feet. In the same instant, Hogarth was aware that Templeton had released Karnes and had grabbed for his gun.

Hogarth whirled toward Templeton, drawing at the same time. The .44 leaped up, and his left hand slapped back across the hammer. The deafening shot seemed to rock the room. It caught Templeton in the shoulder before he could fire, tearing him around and knocking him backward like a heavy blow. He staggered into the window, and the glass shattered in a thousand pieces.

"Hogarth!" Karnes squealed.

He was looking beyond Hogarth, and Hogarth tried to wheel back toward Chapel. But the man had already recovered himself, scooping up the chair to fling it with all his strength. One of the chair legs struck Hogarth in the eye and pain shot through his head. He felt himself staggering backward into the hall, falling. His knuckles rapped against the floor as he hit, and the gun dropped from his numb fingers. Chapel was on him before he could roll over, kicking viciously at his ribs.

Crying out with the pain, Hogarth caught at the boot. He swung Chapel around and threw him heavily against the banister. His body was jack-knifed over the top of it for a moment, and Hogarth used his grip on the man to lift himself up. He had gained his knees before Chapel straightened. As the man tried to kick out again, Hogarth lunged against him with all his weight. The banister popped and crashed and sagged outward. Chapel shouted, pawing wildly at the flimsy frame in a last effort to retain his balance. Hogarth rose to his feet, placing one boot against Chapel's tottering body, grunting as he heaved.

"Hogarth!" screamed Chapel. The banister gave way completely, and he went through it into the stair well. He made a heavy flopping clatter, rolling uncomfortably on down the stairs and coming to a stop on the lower landing.

Barely able to see now, Hogarth whirled at the sound behind him. Templeton was staggering through the door, one hand clutched over his wounded shoulder, his eyes on Hogarth's gun where it lay on the hall floor. Hogarth took one step to kick the gun aside. It put him out from between Templeton and the stairway. He grasped the man by his good shoulder and his belt, spinning him out into the smashed banister. Templeton went through the gap, forced to drop feet first onto the stairway below and crashing against the opposite wall to keep from falling. Hogarth leaped to the head of the stairs.

"You want me to kick you the rest of the way, too?"

Crouched against the wall, clutching his shoulder, Templeton glanced down to where Chapel lay in a moaning heap at the bottom. Then he looked back up at Hogarth. There was murder in his smoky eyes, but he did not move.

Hogarth turned to pick up his gun. He stepped into Karnes's office, closing the door behind him. He still couldn't see out of that one eye, and it hurt like hell.

The obese lawyer stood half way across the room where he had watched the finish of the fight. He stared round-eyed at Hogarth. He tried to grin and failed. He backed up until he was against the desk then took a rumpled handkerchief out to mop sweat from his pasty brow. Finally a strained chuckle left him. He reached up to run his fingers across his face.

"Nice and smooth and whole." The chuckle lost some of its strain. "Nice and fat and smooth. Not a stripe on it. Just like a baby's bottom. I owe you a big vote of thanks, Hogarth. Yes. A big vote."

"You don't have to thank your friends, Oswald."

"Friends?" The man stared at him. He turned his back, circling the desk. He sent a furtive look at Hogarth.

"Would you call Chapel your friend?" Hogarth asked.

The lawyer turned to face Hogarth from behind the desk, fuming and hissing. "That pusillanimous popinjay, that dehydrated dandiprat, that. . . ."

"Please, Oswald," Hogarth said. "Hasn't he suffered enough already?"

The man lost his womanish temper. He pouted again then smiled at Hogarth shyly. "You don't hold it against me then, the way I tried to palm Medicine Wheel Creek off on you?"

"We were all dealing pretty sharp," Hogarth said.

"Sharp is right," chuckled the man. "I never saw such devious machinations outside the bar in all my life. You should have taken to the law, Hogarth."

"Maybe I have, in a way." Hogarth held a palm to his throbbing eye, went over to slouch in the leather chair. He felt the nausea of reaction setting in now. "Do you really think Chapel will bring up that motion to have you voted out?"

Karnes put pudgy hands behind his back, waddled spite-fully around the room. "He can't. He won't dare."

"But if he did, how would it stand? Who could you count on?"

"Kerry, for sure. And Tremaine." The man stopped pacing, frowning, fingering his lips.

"I thought so," Hogarth said. "The Trygvessons don't favor you, do they?"

85

"When they were fighting Kerry's father, in the old days," Karnes said, "there was some suspicion that they were rustling his stock. I handled the case against them."

"And they aren't the kind to forget. So it would be an even vote, Kerry and Tremaine for you, the Trygvessons and Chapel against." Hogarth paused, studying the man's face. "That would leave me in the deciding position, Oswald."

Karnes turned toward him, little eyes wide and round. He started to say something then checked himself, compressing his fat lips. Hogarth smiled, rising from the table.

"It seems sort of a destructive waste, Oswald, for you and me to spend our time outmaneuvering each other. Think what could be accomplished if we worked together. Two clever men, for instance, could prevent anything like that" — he waved a thumb toward the outside stairs — "ever happening again."

"He-he-he." The man began to chuckle. "He-he-he." It bubbled out of him as he turned to pace behind the desk again. He put his hands flat on its top, face wreathed in a grin, still chuckling. "Isn't it a comfortable feeling, Hogarth, when two men reach such a perfect understanding?" His whole body was shaking with his shrill laughter now. "Isn't it a wonderfully comfortable feeling, Hogarth?"

Chapter Seven

Hogarth rode back to his outfit that afternoon with the feeling that he had won at least one man over to his side. He couldn't be sure about Tremaine. The man was friendly enough, but it was a neutral friendliness that would give him no support if he got out on a limb. But he was now sure about Karnes. For his own protection Karnes had to come on Hogarth's side of the fence.

Waco and Simms were both out stringing wire on the new posts and did not return until dusk. Hogarth had dinner nearly ready for them and heard them coming.

But one day he met a man a whole lot badder,
And now he's dead. . . .

"Waco," Simms said disgustedly, "don't you know any more of that song?"

"It's about Billy the Kid."

"You told me that a dozen times. There's a man up in Cody that knows all the songs in the world. You and me are riding up there next Saturday, and he's goin' to teach you the rest of it."

Hogarth stepped out the door to greet the men. They were unsaddling. When the gear was all stripped off, Simms led the two horses down to water. It was then that Waco asked: "Things work out the way you figured?"

"Chapel came in on Karnes," Hogarth said. "So mad he was going to pistol whip the lawyer. I had to break it up. I

87

think I convinced Karnes which side his bread's buttered on."

"You like your new partner?"

"He's a shrewd man."

"Do you *like* him?"

Hogarth glanced irritably at Waco. "How do I know? I've only seen him twice."

"You saw Dagget once and didn't like him. And you were right."

"Let it go, will you? We need Karnes. Isn't that enough?"

Waco did not answer. Hogarth went back in, disturbed by the man's attitude. After they ate, they had a game of stud. But there was a bad taste in Hogarth's mouth. He was restless. He took first watch on the cattle and tried to ride it out. But the question still plagued him. *Do you like Karnes?* He shook his head savagely. *What the hell did it matter?*

The next day they all strung wire. It was hot, and they came home in the afternoon tired and sweaty. A man was waiting, smoking idly in the doorway. It was Joe Hide, one of Kerry Arnold's crew, stubby as a sawed-off scatter gun, with eyes sparkling with mischief and a sackful of the earthiest jokes Hogarth had ever heard. He told them seven in a row and had them howling with laughter before he finally got around to the business that had brought him, letting Hogarth know that Kerry Arnold wanted him over for dinner that evening.

Hogarth shaved and washed and put on clean clothes. It was dusk when he was ready, and a chill wind was already coming down off the mountains. Wearing a blanket coat over his duck jacket, he dropped down out of the high land and came in sight of the Meeteetse lights, winking like fireflies in the darkness. The Big Dipper was a mile north

88

of town, hidden by the grove of poplars till he was almost upon it. The bunkhouse stood a few hundred yards to the south of the main house. Its bottle window spilled a yellow light against Hide's horse, standing outside still under saddle. Hogarth rode up to the big hip-roofed stone house. Instead of a rack there were a dozen cedar posts, each bearing its rusty iron tie ring. He hitched his horse to one and stood for a moment looking up at the imposing, deteriorated building, thinking that in this house had once lived the king of the basin. Then he went up the steps.

A moon-faced Chinese cook greeted him at the front door and led him through a short entrance hall to a great parlor. Immense smoke-blackened beams supported its ceiling. The split, peeled logs lining its walls had been varnished to a high gloss. There was a stone fireplace running the length of one end. Kerry stood before this, with the flames snapping softly behind her and silhouetting her Junoesque figure. Her red hair was done up high. Jade earrings looked almost black against the startling whiteness of her flesh. The dress was a silvery moiré, molded like paint to the upswelling arrogance of her breasts, the lyre flare of her hips. The first sight of her was like a shock, sending a pulse throbbing through Hogarth's body.

"I'm glad you could come. Claret?"

"I drink it on occasion."

"This is an occasion. Ching?"

The Chinese took Hogarth's coat and hat and padded softly from the room. Kerry seated herself in one of the wing chairs by the fireplace. It was upholstered in tapestry, faded and worn by use. Hogarth saw the spur nicks all over the mahogany legs. He took a seat too, glancing around the room.

"It's a beautiful place."

"It *was* a beautiful place," she said.

Ching brought the wine, she poured, and Ching handed a glass to Hogarth. She held her glass a moment, a petulant fullness coming to her lips as she watched him. He thought she was about to make a toast, but she lifted her glass without speaking. She drank and put it on the marquetry table before her. The moiré hissed across her thighs as she leaned back. "What's this about Templeton, now?" she murmured.

"They were going to pistol whip Karnes," he said.

"Quite a coincidence that you happened to be there at the exact moment," she remarked.

"Yes," he murmured. "Wasn't it?"

She studied him, her face utterly sober. Then, surprisingly, she chuckled. She tilted her head back against the chair, and the chuckle became a laugh.

"You're a lot like my father, Hogarth," she said. "Perhaps that's why I like you so much."

Ching announced dinner, and they went to the dining room. Just the two of them by candlelight, with heavy silver service badly tarnished, and cut-glass decanters, and food such as he had never tasted. And wine again in the living room, with only the light of banked coals to see by. They talked of many things. She told him of her life here before her father's death. She spoke of cattle by the tens of thousands grazing over every hill between here and the Mexican border line, of horses so fine that men came from as far away as New York to buy them, of royal parties when the house had rung to the voices of two hundred people, of British noblemen visiting on a hunt. The richest and handsomest men in the state and the most beautiful women had come. Mayors and governors, senators and congressmen, and more than once a President had visited.

A subtle change came over her as she talked. A flush came to her cheeks. Her eyes looked far beyond him, and the firelight made a silvery glitter against their blank surface. When she stopped talking, her eyes remained blank, and she was breathing slowly and deeply.

"You really lived," he said. "You must miss it."

Her head lifted with a snap, as though she had just been wakened from a dream. Her eyes regained focus, and she looked at him almost guiltily. Then she twined her hands in her lap, staring at them.

"No," she said. "Not really."

"Why try to hide it?" he said. "I guess it's really worse to have it and lose it than not to have it at all. It's just too bad you can't get it again, the way things are set up here."

She looked up sharply again. Then she rose and walked to the fire. She seated herself on the shaggy bear rug, arms about her knees.

"You weren't going to talk that way, remember? I knew how it would be when I accepted the idea of this cooperative. It hasn't been so bad, really. Maybe I live more like a sodbuster. But, if this is a good year for the cooperative, I can fix up the house a little, buy a couple of good horses, import a few Black Angus or some whitefaces."

He moved over beside her and sat down. "You make it sound like peanuts."

She turned to him. Their faces were only a few inches apart. "You have ambition yourself," she said.

"Maybe because I was a nobody for so long, and now I've got a chance to become a somebody."

"You are a somebody already, Hogarth." Her voice was husky. "Somebody like this basin has never seen before."

"Is that what you think?"

"That's what I think."

91

She said it in a barely audible whisper, and there was a slumberous provocation to her heavy-lidded eyes. He saw what was there for him to take. And he took it.

He reached out and pulled her to him. She twisted to face him, and the proud shape of her breasts yielded reluctantly to his chest. The taste of passion was on her lips. It pulled the animal things from the pit of him and filled his head with a roaring. When the first kiss was over, he lifted his head away just enough to see her white face. There was a bruised look to her lips, and she was breathing heavily. His voice shook when he spoke.

"If you did this to trap me, you were successful."

"I'd be a fool to pretend I didn't," she said softly.

"All right. Let's talk about the cattle."

"No." She pulled away, rising to her feet. She walked to one end of the mantel, standing with her back to him. "You're only half right. I suppose this was all a setting. The wine and the candlelight. . . ."

"And you."

"Yes." She turned to him with a savage toss of her head. "And me, too. But I think this would have happened anyway. You know it, and I know it."

"Then we understand each other."

"Not completely." The glittering surface was gone from her eyes, and she was all woman for a moment, soft, yielding. "Let's keep it separate, Hogarth. Let's pretend I didn't invite you here to influence you about this cattle deal. Let's pretend it just happened, as it was bound to."

"You mean you don't want to talk about the cattle now?"

"Tomorrow, Hogarth."

He got to his feet too. He gave her a lopsided grin. "I walked into this with my eyes open, Kerry. And now that we understand each other, I think we'd better talk about the cattle. If we wait much longer, we won't have anything to talk about. You were right about the cooperative. I heard Karnes tell Chapel what a spot you're in. Without brood stock for next year, you're through. I knew a couple of those Texas drovers in Cheyenne. One in particular, a man named Frank Cramer. If I guaranteed this check from you, he wouldn't cash it till he got back to Texas. But he's a friend. I don't want to suck him in on a bad deal. If you didn't get the herd through to Standing Rock, if something happened, if you didn't get the government check, where would Cramer stand?"

"He wouldn't get hurt. He'd get his cattle back. He'd slap an attachment on us for the money, and the only way we could pay is by returning his cattle. All he'd be out is a few weeks' time, and he'd lose that anyway, hanging around Cheyenne waiting for another buyer."

Hogarth shook his head. "You make it sound so deceptively simple."

"Stop looking for the joker," she said. "I'm not using my feminine wiles on you now, am I? I'm standing at a respectable distance and discussing a simple business operation as coolly and logically as any businessman would. The whole point is that Cramer won't have to take his cattle back. That government contract is as good as money in the bank. We've driven cattle up there for the last five years without a bobble. The Indian trouble at the agency isn't going to hurt anything. The Indians certainly aren't going to jeopardize the delivery of their only meat supply. It adds up to this . . . if you were Cramer and knew as much about us and about the deal as you do now, would you speculate on it?"

He studied her a moment without speaking. His mind had already been made up before he arrived tonight. After all,

93

Kerry was now only echoing back to him all the things he had said to persuade her to do it in the first place. Now, if Cramer would not get hurt, why not go through with it and get the cattle for Kerry? Looked at cynically, it was no more than a purchase of her friendship. She had hinted as much before.

But now he realized there was more involved. It had got out of hand. They had both lost control of the thing. She had given more than she had planned, and so had he.

"What about Chapel?" he asked.

"He'll sign the check, if he knows we have a man to take it to Cheyenne."

"You'll handle him?"

"Yes."

"The same way you handled me?"

Her head tilted up, green eyes flashing. "What do you want me to say, Hogarth? I thought I was in love with him till you came along. You showed me what a pale imitation of a man he is." She moved toward him, some of the anger fading, an indulgence softening her face. "You hate to think of me in his arms . . . after tonight."

"What did you expect?"

She stopped, inches away. Her mouth had that ripe petulance. "I won't be in his arms, Hogarth. I won't have to be."

His voice was cynical. "Putty in your hands?"

She swayed heavily against him, coming into his arms. Her own arms were about his neck, cool, satiny, demanding. "Don't be like that. What does a man have to fight with? When a man fights, he has his fists or a gun or a dozen other things. A woman has only this. Give me this last time with Chapel. Then I'll tell him exactly how it is. But I've got to have this last time. Could you do it? Could *you* get the check?"

94

The passion of her heavy-lidded eyes and her parted lips was swirling around his head like a scented cloud, and he barely knew what he said. "No. You know it. You know I couldn't get it."

"Then give me this last time. It's our only chance. It's the only way we can save ourselves. We're fighting for it together now, Bob. You know we are."

His kiss blotted out her words.

Chapter Eight

Hogarth did not get back till three in the morning. He slept late and was wakened by Simms, telling him some soldiers were coming. Hogarth pulled on his pants and boots and stepped through the door in his undershirt. A file of blue-clad troopers was riding toward the house. In the lead was a blond young man with a lieutenant's bars on his shoulder straps. The yellow cavalry stripes on his pants winked in the bright sunlight and the musical clatter of scabbards and accouterments floated across the meadow. It drew Waco from the corral behind the house where he had been mending a saddle. The lieutenant checked his bay before the house, dropping his hand in a signal for the troopers to halt. He touched the brim of his forage cap.

"Mister Hogarth?" the lieutenant addressed him.

Hogarth nodded.

"Lieutenant Bannister, Seventh Cavalry. We're down from Standing Rock on the trail of Yellow Elk and some others that left the agency last month."

"A bad Indian?"

"Pretty bad, Mister Hogarth. I was told in town that you'd had a run-in with some Indians in the Big Horns."

"I'm not sure it was Indians, Lieutenant, except for Kasna."

"Charles Tremaine's Crow? I know him. He's all right."

"Otherwise we didn't see anybody else. Just heard this singing. Tremaine said it was the Sioux chant to the sun."

The lieutenant's face darkened. "Where was this?"

96

"Do you know Medicine Wheel?"

Bannister nodded curtly. "Up in the Big Horns. Back toward Hole-in-the-Wall. Is that all you can tell me?"

"About all . . . except that we've noticed the tracks of a barefoot horse around, and some cattle have been cut out. Tremaine didn't seem to think it was done by the Indians you're looking for."

"I'd take his word." Bannister touched his hat brim again. "If you learn any more, I'll be stationed in town for the next few days. I'll appreciate your help."

"Glad to oblige."

The lieutenant lifted his arm, and the troopers came to life, wheeling in file to follow him across the meadow toward the shaggy mountains.

Hogarth and the two men spent the rest of the day mending fences and turned in early. The next morning Kerry rode in alone. She was wearing a dark green divided riding skirt and a white blouse with a golden yellow neckerchief knotted about her slender neck. She had on a flat-crowned tan Stetson with her red hair tucked up beneath it. Both Simms and Waco were in the corral, saddling up, and Hogarth told them to go on without him.

Once they had ridden off, Kerry showed Hogarth the check Chapel had issued, made out to Louis Moffet, the cooperative's cattle buyer in Cheyenne who was to handle the financial aspects of the deal. He was to issue his own check to Frank Cramer, the Texas drover whose name Hogarth had given her as the one waiting in Cheyenne to sell the herd he had brought north, after taking his commission. Her whole face shone with a subdued excitement. She told him he could have Joe Hide and Morry Lucas from her crew to accompany him.

When she left, Hogarth rode out to join the men on the

fences. He found Waco first, digging a posthole. He had his shirt off and sweat ran like rain water off his lean body. Between grunts he told Hogarth that Simms was over the hill, finishing a roll of wire. Hogarth told him what they were going to do. Waco leaned on his shovel, wiping the sweat from his dust-grained brow.

"Sort of rough on Frank Cramer if that government check don't come through, ain't it?"

"I wouldn't do this if I wasn't certain of the government check," Hogarth said. "The Trygvessons and most of the other crews in the cooperative are already shaping up the trail herd for the Indian agencies."

"It's still a gamble, Bobby."

"If anything happens, I will personally drive Cramer's cattle clear back to Texas for him."

"And you would, too. I know you, Bobby. I don't think Cramer has anything to fear. It's you I'm worried about."

"How do you mean?"

"You're selling out, Bobby. I know how bad you want this, but it ain't worth the price you're paying. You needed to be you own boss worse than any man I ever knew. You fought for it all the way up from Texas. Another man might have gone under. A lot of men did. I never saw a man fight harder than you. And it was a good fight. I enjoyed every minute of it. But now it's not good any more. You're compromising. You want it so bad it's blinding you."

"Don't talk that way, Waco."

"I've got to, Bobby. First it was Karnes. Letting Chapel think Karnes blabbed about Dagget to you so you could get Karnes on your side. Why, Bobby? A man you wouldn't have bothered spitting on in the old days. And now it's Kerry Arnold. You've sold out to her on this deal, just as sure as shootin'. You're crawling under the rock with a lot of slimy people just. . . ."

With a sharp curse, Hogarth swung on the man. His fist caught Waco on the side of the jaw and knocked him sprawling. Waco rolled over with a savage sound and came to his hands and knees. Then he stopped, glaring at Hogarth, teeth clamped together so hard the whole ridge of his jaw was knotty with muscle. Hogarth stood with a bleak, taut expression on his face, fists clenched. The only sound in that static moment was the labored wheeze of their breathing.

Then Hogarth opened his hands spasmodically and said: "Damn it, Waco, I'm sorry. I'd give anything to take that back. Give me one. Knock me clear across the pasture."

Waco got to his feet, scrubbing with the heel of one hand at the patches of dirt clinging to his face. "That wouldn't help, Bobby."

Hogarth shook his head helplessly. "You've got all this wrong, Waco. I will admit I went down there with the idea of winning Kerry over to our side. But it's gone farther than that now. Too much farther. That's why I was so proddy, I guess. A man can't take that kind of talk about his woman."

Waco frowned at him. "It's that serious?"

Hogarth's lips compressed. "It is."

"Even more than Elaine?"

"There's no comparison."

Still frowning intensely, Waco walked over to the shovel, picked it up. He slouched there, feet spread widely apart, holding the shovel, staring off at the mountains.

The somber expression on his face made Hogarth ask: "You drifting?"

"Because of that punch?" Waco asked, still not looking at him.

"It was a helluva thing to do."

99

Waco slowly turned to face him. "You want me to go?"

"Hell, no. You know that."

"Then I guess I ain't drifting. I couldn't walk out on you when you need me most, Bobby."

"Now what do you mean by that?"

"Let it go, will you? I'm staying."

"All right. If you'll ride to Cheyenne with me . . . I need you. That is the only chance the cooperative has of staying alive. You've got Kerry wrong in this."

"Maybe I have," Waco said. "Anyway, I'll go south with you."

They left the next morning. Simms stayed behind to watch the Rocker T with the responsibility puffing him up like a bantam. They took four of his quarter horses for a saddle string and picked Morry Lucas and Joe Hide up at Kerry's and strung out for Cheyenne. Joe Hide joked all the way down and had Waco out of his bad mood by the second day. He knew every girl in every town along the way, and they all loved him. He and Waco went on a rip-roaring drunk in Anchor, won fifty dollars in a poker game from the mayor of Casper, and fought seven cowpokes to a standstill at Muskrat. Waco swore he'd never had such a high-heel time, and he and Joe were just going to keep on riding and never stop.

At Cheyenne they went looking for more fun, while Hogarth bought the cattle. Frank Cramer had 950 steers, but he was tired of waiting around for quotations to go up. Hogarth was able to beat him down to four dollars a head.

Hogarth had been wondering whether Moffet might, on an off chance, wire Cody for confirmation on the cooperative's check. However, it would take two days for the Cody bank to send a man to Meeteetse to clear the cooperative account, and Moffet apparently had too much faith in the

100

cooperative and was too hungry for a deal after such a low period to take the chance of losing the commission that such a delay might cause. Cramer himself was a veteran in the cattle business. He had been selling Moffet feeders since the early 'Seventies and was steeped in the off hand, casual way of doing business that was a tradition with the old-time cattlemen where a man's word was his bond. Moffet endorsed the cooperative's check, that carried Hogarth's okay on it, and then issued his own check to Frank Cramer. The cattleman was satisfied, and it was a closed deal.

Hogarth hunted for Joe Hide and Waco till after two o'clock in the morning before he found them dead drunk in an alley behind the Frontier Saloon. He and Lucas dragged them around front and dumped them in the water trough. Then they took the drenched, staggering men to the Texas Cafe and forced a quart of black coffee down each of them. At five they were at the bed grounds outside of town, getting the cattle on their feet, pushing them into the broken land north of town.

It was no high-hell time going back. They drove early and late, through the same big mountains, the Laramies, the Rattlesnakes, the Wind Rivers. Three hundred miles as the crow flies and probably twice that much by trail. Altogether it required almost a full month of dust and heat, hunger and rain, and at the end the men were exhausted and the cattle spooky. By the time they reached Meeteetse, Hogarth had lost fifteen pounds and was ringy enough to eat off the same plate with a snake.

He knew the Trygvessons would probably be gone up north with the cooperative's trail herd. But he didn't know whether Chapel and Tremaine had gone with them. Not wanting a clash till he checked with Kerry Arnold on how they stood, he left the herd ten miles south of the basin and rode alone to the Big Dipper. She answered the knock at the door. He had that first stunning picture of her — the dark blue of her watered silk dress in sharp contrast to the white flesh of her face and arms, the daylight burning rustily against the tiara of her hair. Her eyes were wide with surprise and relief.

"We did it," he said.

Triumph flushed her face and gave her eyes a jeweled sparkle. Then she caught him with both hands and pulled him inside. Without closing the door, without removing his hat, he took her in his arms. She wheeled her back toward the wall beside the door, and he pinned her there, kissing her with a hunger born of six womanless weeks on the trail. She sobbed with the passion of it and met his hunger savagely.

She let him drink deeply but not deeply enough. When the first fury abated, she swung aside and away from him. She still held his hands, pulling him back into the room. Her round breasts swelled with each panting breath she took, and the excitement still flushed her cheeks. She pulled him down on the couch, sitting beside him without coming into his arms again.

"We're still not out of the woods," she said. "The Trygvessons should be back with the government check soon. But I don't want them to hear about this until the check is actually on deposit here. Then they won't be able to do anything to jeopardize the deal."

"They wouldn't be fool enough to foul things up when they have the money in their hands to cover that check."

"Wouldn't they? You've seen how blind Sigrod is. If word of this got to him before the check left his possession, he'd know we got it on speculation. I wouldn't put it past him to tear up that check simply because we bucked him."

Hogarth leaned back, remembering the blindness of the old man's anger as he had sat in the middle of Main Street that morning on the white stallion. "I suppose you're right." He frowned, shaking his head. She asked him what was the matter. "I don't know," he said. "I've just never had to put on a juggling act like this before."

"How can you still doubt," she said, "when you've pulled it off? You've saved us all, Hogarth. It might even be the thing that will win the Trygvessons over to your side . . . when they realize what it really means."

She was in his arms again, with the words blurred as they kissed, the world spinning around him in the scent of her and the sound of her and the feel of her. But again, it was not enough. She was twisting free, standing up.

"I want you to stay more than anything. But Tremaine's coming. We can't take a chance now, Hogarth."

He let her pull him up, catching her again. "When, then? When?"

She gave him another kiss, let her lips slide across his cheek till the passionately whispered words were in his ear. "Soon. As soon as possible. I'll try to ride up to see you. Don't come down again. We can't take the chance of somebody seeing you."

"You make it rough."

"A little while longer, darling. Only a little while."

He got back to the herd after nightfall, with the intense frustration still burning through him. He had turned over to Kerry the money that was left from the check he'd floated and inside himself he knew she was right. He knew they couldn't take a chance, now that they were so close to success. He had the men drive the herd the last ten miles that night, reaching the eastern end of the Rocker T near dawn. They scattered the cattle in little bunches through the pockets tucked into the first shaggy jaws of the mountains. The beef wouldn't require much herding here, just watching, and they pitched a half-faced camp high on the slope. They were all out of coffee, bacon, even cigarette makings. Hogarth left the three men in camp and rode down to the Rocker T for fresh supplies.

It gave him the feeling of coming home to see Simms's quarter horses milling around in the corral behind the house, to smell the resin and pitch of wood smoke lacing the air. The sun was up, burning hotly against the front of the log building, and Simms opened the door with a bullhide bucket in his hand just as Hogarth rode up. He was beside himself with joy, pulling Hogarth off his horse and clapping him on the back.

"I thought you'd done gone and left me to them barefoot pony tracks and them damn' Swedes. Where's that seven-foot Davy Crockett rail from Texas?"

Hogarth grinned broadly. "Up watching some beef we brought back. I came down to get them some grub."

"I shot a buck yesterday, and the steaks are right out of heaven," Simms said. "You eat. I'll take them their grub."

Simms unwrapped the venison steaks and threw two of them in the frying pan. The coffee was already made, and Hogarth poured himself a cup. It scalded his mouth, but it revived him.

Rubbing red-rimmed eyes, he asked: "What was that about the barefoot pony tracks?"

Simms kicked another log into the fire, frowning. "I didn't want to say nothing till you had a full belly. They been around."

"Lost any cattle?"

The man scowled, scratching at his leathery jowls.

"Hogarth, I watched those cattle like babies, nighthawked all the time. . . ."

"How many?"

The man spat, spoke reluctantly. "One, as far as I made out."

Hogarth threw his head back to laugh. It was the first good laugh he'd had in weeks. Simms frowned at him, and Hogarth leaned out to punch him affectionately in the belly.

"You're a good man, Shorthorse. Don't worry about losing one steer. We couldn't even stop it when we were all here." He took another gulp of coffee. "How about that lieutenant? Did he ever find Yellow Elk?"

"Not hide nor hair. Lieutenant Bannister's still around. He staked out that Medicine Wheel thing for weeks, but he never saw nothing. Now he's up north around Cody with some Crow trackers, trying to find Yellow Elk's camp."

Hogarth sloshed the coffee around in his cup, staring at it. "And while he's gone, the barefoot tracks show up?"

The man flipped the sizzling venison steaks, squinting. "That's right. I see what you're driving at. Whoever it is must hole up when those soldiers are around. The last time it hit, Bannister was down around Casper, checking some farmer's story that he'd seen a war party."

"How long ago?"

"More'n a month, I'd say."

"Throw some makings in that pack, too. We been without cigarettes a week."

Simms put his sack of Bull Durham and a book of cigarette papers into the saddle bags along with the sack of venison steaks and salt rising bread. Then he hoisted the saddle on a broad shoulder and took it outside.

Hogarth undressed slowly, trying to add it up. Why should the rider on the barefoot horse take only one steer from the

Rocker T herd when he took a dozen or more steers from the others in the Basin? He could find no answer and fell asleep still thinking about it.

He slept all day and most of the next night, waking a little before dawn. He rode up to where Waco and the others were camped, finding that nothing had occurred. He stayed with them and helped on the watches. For three days nothing happened. Kerry Arnold did not show up. There was not even word from her. Hogarth was growing edgy with the desire to see her and to wind this up. On the third evening Joe Hide nighthawked from ten till two. About one in the morning he woke Hogarth to tell him he'd found fresh barefoot tracks near the herd.

Hogarth was not surprised. The soldiers were gone, and it had been almost five weeks. It was a logical time for the tracks to show up. He told Hide ruefully that he felt as if he were welcoming an old friend.

They waked the others. Hogarth sent Waco and Lucas to high ridges where they could watch the herd. Then Hide led Hogarth to the spot. The prints led through a bunch of steers bedded down in a cañon, then ran on up the cañon into the mountains. One steer had been taken.

"You stay here," Hogarth said. "It'll take all three of you to hold this herd if something happens. If I'm not back in the morning, don't worry. This is the hottest trail we've had, and it may take me a long way."

Even in the bright moonlight, it was slow work. He was off his horse half the time and still lost the trail frequently. Then he had to backtrack and circle and use every other device he had learned in a lifetime of this kind of work. When the moon died, he had to wait till dawn, shivering in the chill. Then the daylight came, and he could push faster. The sun rose, warming him, and he found himself climbing through mountains bursting with early summer.

The chokeberries were darkening from red to black along the stream beds, and the pools were covered with fluffy cottonwood tufts that began dropping this time of year. White-tailed deer bounced away from him through the pines; marmots whistled on sun-burnished rocks; chipmunks heckled him all along his trail. He passed a small lake with moose feeding belly-deep in its marshes. Mosquitoes flushed out of the willows like wisps of smoke, fretting the horse till the lake was left behind. He was beyond the headwaters of Medicine Wheel Creek and deep in the somber mountains when he again came in sight of the bald peak.

He halted his horse a moment, staring at the mountain. There was not even a wind to rustle the branches. The dead silence was like a thin pressure, growing against him. He felt it brush through the primitive corners of him.

The sudden crashing sound swept against him like a blow. The quarter horse shied aside, and Hogarth wheeled in the saddle, yanking at his saddle gun. He had it half free of the scabbard, fighting to hold the horse at the same time, when a shaggy brown bear broke free of the berry bushes and halted in surprise. It stood there a moment, blinking reddened eyes at him. Then, with a disgusted snort, it turned and lumbered away.

Hogarth quieted the horse, grinning wryly. Urging with his knees, he now heeled the animal on toward the peak. He passed into high timber, reaching the trail they had been on when they had been shot at before. He crossed it and went up to the ridge, keeping to the cover of the rocks and scrub timber. He searched the head of the valley below for the first sign of that primitive stone wheel. Before he saw it, he heard the sound. It was the same sound, high and eerie. There was something weird about it — in all the vast silence — something that made his skin crawl. He dropped down from dense timber, then dismounted, slipping his Ward-Burton out of its scabbard. Slowly he began to work his way toward the sound.

Wanks tan han he ya u we lo
Wanks tan han he ya u we lo. . . .

He could see the prehistoric shrine now, with its spokes of immense limestone blocks. He moved more carefully down through the juniper, the tamarack, the pine. He could see the huge block that constituted the hub of the wheel, with the chalky buffalo skull on top of it. And before it, kneeling, facing that skull, was the chanter. The figure was crouched down, head thrown back, arms spread out to the sun above, the high-pitched voice rising and falling in that monotonous, eerie chant.

Mita we cohan tapa wan la
Ka nu we he ya u we lo. . . .

Hogarth reached the edge of the timber. Wild hawks splashed their crimson patches across an emerald meadow that rolled down to the flats where the wheel was laid out. Hogarth could see the figure more clearly now, ink-black hair falling against the back of a white doeskin jacket. There was a horse ground-hitched half way down one of the spokes of the wheel — a pinto pony. Beyond the horse, picketed to a tree with a rawhide rope, stood a steer with Frank Cramer's Dizzy Circle vented brand on its flank.

Hogarth would be exposed as soon as he left timber, but the chanter's back was to him. There was no wind to carry his scent to the horse and steer. He had to take the chance. He moved out into the haws, crouched low, hands tightly on the Ward-Burton.

Anpe wi kin he ya we lo
A ye ye ye yo. . . .

He reached one end of the spoke, ducked behind the first huge limestone block. From here he moved to the next one. They were higher than his waist and afforded adequate cover as long as he kept low. The doeskin jacket on the chanter made him think of Kasna. Hadn't Tremaine's Indian worn one when they had found him here before?

His darting motion between the slabs of limestone must have attracted the pinto's attention. The horse tossed his head and snorted. The chanting ceased abruptly. Hogarth knew that he had to make the break now and jumped into the open. The figure of the singer was thirty feet ahead of him, turned his way, half risen. Hogarth almost stopped, catching his breath in surprise. It was a woman.

Chapter Nine

They gaped blankly at each other, both gripped by the same surprise. Then the girl wheeled and darted toward the pinto. Hogarth recovered, running toward the horse, too. She reached it first, running up behind and vaulting over its rump into the saddle. It was an Indian way of mounting, the same thing he had seen her do that first evening when she had tried to cut a steer from their herd. The pinto bolted as soon as she hit the saddle.

Hogarth was almost upon them by then. She tried to veer aside and run the animal through an opening between two of the limestone blocks comprising one of the spokes. He threw himself at the horse, dropping his rifle and catching one of the girl's legs as the pinto lunged past. He pulled her out of the saddle, and she pitched down on top of him, with the horse running on through the opening in the slabs.

The weight of her coming against him knocked the breath from Hogarth as he struck the ground. He felt her soft body sprawled across him, then felt her scrambling off. Gasping for air, he caught her arm. She screamed like a cat and clawed for his face. He had to release her to ward off the sharp nails. Again she tried to scramble free. He made another wild grab, and his hand tangled in that swirl of ink-black hair.

Holding to it, he twisted her off and then rolled over to his knees. She tried to roll away, but he jerked her back by her hair. She tried it again, cried out in pain at the sharp tug on her hair, and rolled back and subsided. Her face was contorted and she spat at him in rage: *"Can'l wanka, winkete, wablenical!"*

The humor of it struck him, and he had to grin. "I wish I knew what that meant, honey. It sounds pretty bad."

"It means 'coward,' " she stormed. "It means 'man-woman.' It means 'man-without-parents.' It means the worst name I can think of for you."

She finally ran down, staring up at him from sullen black eyes. They didn't have the Indian opacity that Kasna's held. Instead it was a smoky blackness, filled with the promise of a dozen hues. Her skin looked almost white, yet there was a coppery tint to it in the hollows beneath the high, slanting cheekbones. Her lips were full and pouting with her violent anger, and as red as chokeberries.

"I'll let go of your hair if you promise not to run."

"I won't promise."

He grinned at her. "Then we'll sit this way for a while."

She gave an angry tug, gasped at the pain, subsided once more.

He stared down at her, flat on her back beside him. "It's hard to believe it was you, cutting out all those cattle," he said.

"Cutting?"

"Rustling. Stealing."

"I took only what we . . . what I had to eat."

"A dozen at a crack is a lot to eat."

"I never took that many. Just one at a time."

He fished the cylindrical cherry-wood case from his pocket. "I'll give you this if you'll promise not to run."

She stared at it then reached up involuntarily. *"Wotahe . . . !"* He pulled it out of her reach, still pinning her by her hair to the ground. Her pupils began to distend again. But her eyes were still on the cherry-wood case. Finally, sul-

111

lenly, she said: "I promise."

He let her sit up and handed over the case.

"You dropped it the first time you hit our herd. It must mean a lot to you."

"Wotahe!" she cried, clutching at it. She pulled it to her, stifling the momentary joy beneath that sullen defiance again. "It's my bird man. The boys carry other charms. It protects us from harm."

A small grin touched his lips. He ran his thumb across his teeth in the absent-minded, speculative gesture, studying her. "What do they call you?"

"Wastewin," she said. "I guess you'd say it meant Pretty Face."

"Well, Pretty Face," he muttered, "where did you get your English?"

"They had a mission school at Pine Ridge Agency."

"You're a little south of your pasture, aren't you?"

Her whole slim body grew rigid, and her face darkened with a strange, new, bitter rage that shook her voice hoarsely.

"There is no agency now. There is no tribe. Crazy Horse was murdered at Fort Robinson. My whole family was killed at Wounded Knee. A hundred other Ghost Dancers were killed there. The Lakotas are scattered all over the Big Horns now."

He moved a thumb toward the buffalo skull. "This some sort of war dance you been pulling here?"

"The Song of the Sun," she said. "The braves are dead or fighting now. They cannot perform the Sun Dance. Someone must do it. I prayed to Wakan Tanka that we would find freedom."

"I'm sorry," he said.

"I want no pity."

"All right," he said. "Standing Rock. That's where Yellow Elk ran off from, isn't it?"

She did not answer. She stared back at the little cherry-wood case, her lips pouting sullenly. It made her look like a little girl. He realized how long he had been hunkered down beside her. He rose to his feet, tucking his thumbs into his Levi pockets.

"If you're part of Yellow Elk's bunch, Lieutenant Bannister will want to see you. I'll take you into town."

"No!" She jumped to her feet, eyes wild. "I will not go!"

She wheeled, as if to run. Instead of lunging after her, he called sharply: "You gave me your word. Is the word of a Sioux worthless?"

She stopped. She stood rigidly, breathing heavily. Her weight finally settled against the ground. There was an intense plea on her face.

"Please. Not into town."

"I've got to, honey. This rustling's got to stop."

"But I only took one steer at a time, just for food."

"Sometimes it was more than that, and all on a barefoot horse. I'd like to believe you. But how do I know? If you'd tell me everything, maybe it would clear you."

Her head lowered till she was staring blankly, stubbornly at the ground.

He said: "Let's go get your horse, then."

He saw her head snap up again, saw the wild look in her eyes, and knew that not even her promise would hold her now. He jumped after her this time as she whirled, catching her by an arm before she could bolt. She fought him and he caught her other arm, holding her writhing body to him.

"You'd better decide right now," he said. "Quiet down and you can ride in. Keep this up and I'll hog-tie you and throw you over the back of your horse."

113

She stopped fighting. Her head twisted over one shoulder in an effort to see him. She bit her lip in savage anger, her body rigid. Finally she said: "All right."

He let her go, watching warily. She made no effort to run. He moved his thumb toward the limestone blocks. She walked slowly between two of them, in the direction the pinto had taken. From here they saw that the spooked pony had stopped up by the fringe of timber. They walked to it. Hogarth saw an old Sharps rifle lashed with thongs to the buffalo saddle. He put his hand on it.

"Somebody took a shot at us, too, the last time we were up here."

She spoke with her head lowered. "I was only trying to drive you away. I thought you were after me." Her voice grew lower. "Now I wish I had aimed at you."

He took up the rawhide reins and led the pinto through the timber to where his horse was. Then he took the reins off and made a lead rope out of them, so she would have no control over the pinto. Face flushed, she stepped into the buffalo saddle. He mounted his short horse, holding the lead rope of the pinto, and went back to turn the steer loose. Then, driving it ahead of them, they turned west.

It was late afternoon when they dropped out of the last hoary shoulders of the Big Horns and onto the foot slopes above Medicine Wheel Creek. The lodgepoles here grew a hundred feet tall and were crisscrossed with old scars made by moose and deer rubbing the velvet from their antlers. The late sun filled the timber with a close heat, its light lying like gold along the endless aisles of pine and spruce.

They were on the Meeteetse Trail, crossing the last ridge before it dropped into the flatlands, when they caught sight of the two riders below. Hogarth recognized them almost immediately by their size. He had an impulse to pull back

114

into timber. But he knew that they had already seen him. He drew his horse to a stop. He wanted to remain above them.

They pushed their immense horses up the slope at a steady, plodding walk. The one in the lead was Otherre, Sigrod's eldest son. The one following him was Are, the youngest. They pulled their horses to a halt five feet from Hogarth, looking up the steep slant of the trail at him.

"How long have you been back?" Hogarth asked.

Otherre was looking at the woman. His flat-topped hat was chalky with trail dust, and his hair hung in a yellow mane clear to his shoulders. "We got back yesterday," he said.

"Any trouble?"

"Not about the money, if that's what you mean. We deposited the government check in the bank before we found out about the cattle you bought without any money." There was a glacial anger in Otherre's pale blue eyes. "My father was right about you, Hogarth. Even Kerry would not have been as sly and underhanded as that."

"Even Kerry. . . !" Hogarth checked himself in time. He did not speak again. Let them think what they wanted. It would all come out in time.

Otherre nodded his shaggy head at the girl. "Who is this one?"

"I found her at Medicine Wheel."

Otherre frowned at him, then he shifted his weight to get off his horse. All the Trygvessons rode imported Texas Porters, the heaviest saddles they could get. Hogarth saw the strands of hair on the front girth separate with the strain as the man stepped off. He walked ponderously to the pinto and bent to lift its foreleg. The horse snorted, shifting away, but he made it lift the hoof. Then he dropped it, straightening, and turned to Hogarth.

"So she is the rustler."

"I don't know yet."

"How did you know she was at Medicine Wheel?"

"I didn't."

"You would not ride that far for pleasure. You were trailing her, is that it? A rider on an unshod horse, rustling some of your cattle. And you followed the tracks and found her there."

They had the picture. There was no use covering it up. "She only took one of my steers," he said.

"She took twenty of ours. More than once."

"How do you know it was her?"

Are shifted angrily in his saddle. "Don't be a fool. Who else could it be? That lieutenant was down here hunting Yellow Elk before we left. Did he find him?"

Hogarth glanced at Are. The young man had obviously tried to grow a beard on the trip north, but it was still little more than a yellow fuzz. "No," Hogarth said. "Lieutenant Bannister didn't find Yellow Elk."

"She must be one of them, then," Are said. "We'd better take her to Father."

"You aren't taking her anywhere," Hogarth said.

Otherre reached up to run a thumb roughly through his own inch-long beard. The gesture revealed his knuckles to Hogarth again, scarred and swollen from some old breakage. Hogarth wondered if the damage had come from hitting a man.

"My father has long wanted to find out who is doing this rustling, Hogarth," Otherre said. "And now we come back to find out that you bought cattle in Cheyenne without authorization, without even money in the bank to cover the check. My father is in a great rage about it. You would be a fool to antagonize him further. We will take the woman."

"And work her over, maybe, if she didn't talk soon enough."

Are slapped a grimy hand against his saddle horn. "The Trygvessons know how to treat a woman."

"That's what I'm afraid of."

A long-tailed cat began to cackle from a tree somewhere behind them. Are put his reins against the neck of his horse. It started edging toward Hogarth's flank. Otherre let his scarred hand drop to his side. His eyes looked like chipped glass.

"Keep your horse where it is," Hogarth said.

Are pulled his reins in, checking the horse abruptly. He glanced at Otherre, as if for instructions. Otherre was still looking at Hogarth. Wastewin was watching Hogarth, too. Her eyes were wide and black, her lips parted. Otherre's glance slid down to the oiled oak stock of Hogarth's six-shooter. Hogarth knew what was going through the man's mind. Everyone in the basin knew what had happened to Lee Dagget at Chapel's ranch and to Templeton in Karnes's office.

Hogarth was looking at Otherre's big, brutal hands. The tendons in the wrists were as big around as Hogarth's little finger. The calluses made thick pads on the fingers. They would not be fast with a gun.

Otherre raised his eyes to Hogarth's face once more. The wind died down. For a moment it was utterly silent.

"Take the woman, Hogarth. You will not have her long."

Chapter Ten

The sky was crimson with sunset when they reached Meeteetse. Window glass flashed and glittered at Hogarth from every building as he led the girl down Main Street. The crowd of idlers before Gilroy's stable turned to gape then began to dribble after him. Doc Powdre came out onto his balcony in his shirt sleeves and put both hands on the rail to lean and stare at the riders. Ab Kidder came up from his tilted chair in front of the general store and walked to the edge of the porch.

"What you got there, Hogarth? Looks like an Injun."

Hogarth wanted to get Wastewin off the street before a crowd formed. He didn't know exactly what their temper would be and didn't want to take a chance.

"Get the marshal for me, will you, Ab?" he said. "We'll be in Oswald Karnes's office."

He stepped down before the Big Horn Building, hitching his reins to the rack. Wastewin slid off, glancing apprehensively at the men coming out of the saloon and walking over from the stable. He saw the rigid line to her body and moved in close.

"Run now and you'll only make it worse. You're safer with me."

She sent him a venomous glance then walked ahead of him into the building. The stairs made a hollow clatter under his boots. The door to Oswald Karnes's office was open, and he let Wastewin enter first. Karnes was not there. But Kerry Arnold was.

She stood beside the window Templeton had broken when he had fallen back from Hogarth's bullet. She had on a suede riding habit and a dark green shirt that made her white skin stand out in vivid contrast. By comparison, Wastewin looked like a sullen, dirty child.

"What have we here?" Kerry asked.

"I found her up at Medicine Wheel," Hogarth said. "She was riding a barefoot pony."

Kerry glanced sharply at him, as if trying to read what was in his face. "What should that mean?"

"Let's get our cards on the table, Kerry. Somebody on an unshod horse has been cutting cattle out of the cooperative herds in small bunches. Tremaine and Chapel and the Trygvessons have suffered. Surely you weren't overlooked."

A little flutter of expression ran through her face. She half turned away, frowning. "I suppose not, Hogarth."

"You never mentioned it."

"It only happened to me since you came, and that's when you were down in Cheyenne. It's been such a strange business, Hogarth. None of us could figure it out. Tremaine swore no Indians would operate like that." She stopped, looking at Wastewin again. "What has she told you?"

"She admitted she cut out cattle. But she claims it's only one at a time, for food."

"One at a time." Kerry sounded disgusted. She walked over to Wastewin, her skirts swinging spitefully. Her voice was cold, and her chin was high. "It would be much easier for you if you came out with the whole thing. Are you part of Yellow Elk's band?"

There was a square, obstinate shape to Wastewin's lower lip. She met Kerry's gaze with blank eyes. Hogarth could see how it infuriated Kerry.

He said: "She wouldn't answer me, either. The best thing

119

we can do is wait for Lieutenant Bannister to come back. He'll probably know if she's with Yellow Elk, might even know her well enough to get her to talk. In the meantime I think we'd better put her in the custody of the marshal. I know there's feeling against these rustlers. The Trygvessons have already threatened me."

Kerry turned sharply to him. "You saw them?"

"Are and Otherre. They said Sigrod had already found out about the Cheyenne deal."

"He did. He almost blew up. If he hadn't already banked the government check, I think he would have destroyed it. But there's nothing he can do now. The government money covers Moffet's check to Cramer and our check to Moffet, and the cattle are ours." She looked at him, smiling thinly, her eyes shining. "It's really quite a triumph, Hogarth. Sigrod is a good man . . . in his way. But he's got a stubborn, pig-headed, miserly streak in him that's kept the cooperative from developing into what it should be . . . for years. This is the first time I've been able to get past him. But I think my position is proven to the other members now, and they won't let Trygvesson block the more progressive ideas I have any longer."

There was a clatter on the stairs, and Ab Kidder appeared on the landing. "Marshal's not in his office."

Hogarth frowned at him. "Look across town, then. You can cover it in ten minutes."

"I don't think that would do any good," the storekeeper said. "Templeton just came in from the Meeteetse Trail. He saw all four of the Trygvessons coming this way. They'll want that Indian if she's in on this rustling."

"What's that got to do with the marshal?"

"I guess he didn't want to stand up to the Trygvessons, Hogarth."

120

Hogarth glanced at Kerry, and she nodded, saying, "That's about it."

"But we can't just turn her over to the Trygvessons, Kerry."

"Don't make it sound so terrible. I told you, Sigrod isn't so bad . . . underneath."

"It's not a matter of bad or good. It's what he's like when he's mad. I've seen that, Kerry."

"He wouldn't do anything."

"How do you know? I saw a mob lynch a rustler once. I saw one man whip them up to it."

"But not a woman, not even if she is one of the rustlers."

"How do you know, Kerry? You said Sigrod was ready to bust a gut over that cattle deal. What's he capable of? A man like that . . . primitive . . . animal . . . in a rage?"

Through the broken window they heard a new sound from outside, a drumming of hoofs, a shouting. Kerry walked to the window, looked down into the street. Her face grew bleak.

"It looks like you'll have a chance to find out."

Hogarth went swiftly to stand beside her. He saw the four riders coming down the street. The leader was riding a huge white stallion, speckled with dirty yellow lather. He was hatless, and his long white hair whipped like a banner in the wind. Hogarth wheeled to grasp Kerry's elbow.

"Do as I say now. I'm not turning her over to them. I'm going to meet them in the Bullhorn. That will give you a chance to get the girl out the back of this building. I'll send Jigger to the livery stable for horses. Get Wastewin out the back way to your ranch and keep her there till you hear from me, or till Bannister comes back."

"Hogarth," Kerry said, "you can't meet them alone. Not over that Indian. You've played it so smart up to now, don't throw it all away for this . . . not for a dirty little Indian woman you never saw before. It isn't the time, Hogarth, it isn't the time."

"On the contrary." He wheeled away from the window, looking at Wastewin. Her eyes were wide and black, and an intense pallor had taken the sun tint from her face. "Whether it's my choosing or not, this *is* the time."

Chapter Eleven

A miniature whirlwind was forming. It picked up a funnel of saffron dust on the west side of Main Street and pirouetted it across the twisted ruts and deposited it against the splintered curbing of the east side. But it was no longer working in silence. The plank walk shuddered to high-heeled boots. A second story window slammed up.

"What is it, Harry?" called the man up there.

"The Trygvessons," shouted the man, running down the walk. "They're coming in on something."

Jimmy Furgusson jumped out the door of the store, upturning a basket of apples. They rolled off into the street with a subdued clatter. Someone shouted to Furgusson from the barbershop. It was into this hubbub that Hogarth stepped from the stairway. He halted just within, to place the horsemen, only a block away now. Then he ran across the sidewalk to his horse and darted across the street from behind the animal toward the Bullhorn, hoping the Trygvessons would figure he had just dismounted.

"Hogarth!" roared Sigrod, his voice rumbling down the street like shattered icebergs.

Hogarth had already gained the saloon, shoving through the batwing doors. There were two cowhands at the bar, and they backed toward the rear door, a wary surprise stiffening their saddle-bound figures.

"Jigger," panted Hogarth. "Send your swamper to Gilroy's Livery. Have him take two horses over behind the Big Horn Building. Don't let those Swedes see him."

"Got you," said Jigger, his eyes round and frightened. Tearing off his apron, he ran toward the back end, shouting for the half-breed swamper.

The unmistakable sounds of running horses being hauled to their haunches out front came through the batwings. The sidewalk clattered to the heavy passage of boots. Then the doors were flung wide to slam against the walls, and Sigrod Trygvesson came through them like an angry bull.

"That's all," said Hogarth, and he was not wearing his Mackinaw.

Sigrod stopped with his eyes pinned to Hogarth's hand held stiffly out to his side.

"If I pull it, I'll use it."

"Are is at the window with a shotgun, Hogarth," said Sigrod. "If you make to pull that thing, you'll get both charges. You know what we're after. Is she here?"

"What makes you want her so badly?" Hogarth demanded.

"She's in with this rustling," said Sigrod. "What makes you so eager for her defense?"

"I figure your methods of interrogation won't suit a lady," replied Hogarth.

"She's no lady," said Sigrod. "She's no better than any other long rider we catch. We'd string them up." Sigrod began moving toward him, his massive shoulders swaying from side to side slightly with each deliberate, inexorable step. "Is she in here, Hogarth?"

Rane and Otherre had come in behind their father, and they spread out so Hogarth could see them both and their intent. He felt the small beads of sweat pop out on his forehead.

"I said you don't get her," he told them quietly.

"If you've got her here, we will," insisted Sigrod. "You said you'd fight for a good reason, Hogarth. I hope you think this

is a good reason because, by Thor, you're going to fight. . . ."
— and the last escaped him in a hoarse, deafening bellow
as his prodigious frame gathered itself and erupted toward
Hogarth — *"Siger!"*

Hogarth was standing where the cowhands had been
drinking their beer, and he reached out his left hand and
swept both heavy glasses off the bar at Sigrod's face. The
man was coming in too fast to avoid them, and one of the
glasses struck him fully in the mouth. Sigrod shouted
spasmodically with the pain and was blinded for a moment,
so that he could not see the direction Hogarth took toward
him and was in no position to block it.

Hogarth dived under Sigrod's arms, and his shoulder
struck the man's belly. It was like hitting a pig of galena
lead. Hogarth heard his own gasp of pain. But he had
calculated his position to take Sigrod off-balance, and his
feet churned the floor like pistons, driving on in.

Sigrod's momentum would not allow him to be stopped by
Hogarth's smaller body. It knocked him off to the side, and
that momentum carried him on till he pounded into a table.
Both of them went over on the upturning table, crashing to
the floor in a bedlam of yells and splintering wood.

Hogarth writhed free of the welter and rolled to his feet
with the blinding catty speed of which he was so capable.
He was whirling to catch Sigrod coming up when he heard
the hoarse shouts behind him. It did not surprise Hogarth.
Perhaps Sigrod had meant Rane and Otherre to stay out of
it, but the sight of battle unleashed primitive Viking emotions they could not control.

"What did I tell you!" roared Sigrod.

It did not stop the two sons. Sigrod was clawing his way
onto his feet up the tilting top of the overturned deal table.
Hogarth caught one of its legs and crouched down to heave

upward. The table went over, and Sigrod fell onto his back beneath it with a shrill curse. Hogarth whirled back, catching a chair as he went and allowing his whirling motion to carry it on around in an arc at the end of his arm. He released it at the end of the arc, and the chair skidded across the floor into Otherre, taking the man's feet from beneath him. The whole room shuddered with his crashing fall.

Hogarth was already running at Rane, as if he meant to meet him upright. A savage satisfaction lit Rane's face when he saw this. But Hogarth knew what a mistake it would be to pitch his inferior bulk against the man like that. In the last instant he threw himself downward, twisting to one side. Rane tried to shift away from it but was coming forward too fast. Hogarth struck him across the knees with the whole side of his body. Rane went down across him, and they both slid across the floor to come up against the bar.

Again it was Hogarth's speed that counted. He rolled away from the huge man and got his feet beneath him. He heard Otherre and Sigrod coming in from behind and knew this had to be good. Rane pawed at the floor for support to rise. Hogarth kicked him in the head. It knocked Rane's face into the bar with a soft thud. The man emitted a sick sound and tried to rise again. Hogarth gave him a second, vicious kick. The man made no sound this time but still tried to come up. Hogarth lashed out a third time with all his brutal capacity. Rane's face went into the side of the bar again, and he stayed that way.

Hogarth had already tried to whirl away, but Otherre was rushing in too fast. He felt a propulsive, irresistible weight strike his body, and was carried into the bar beside Rane. Hogarth screamed with the terrible pain. For a moment he was paralyzed and thought his back had been broken.

He felt Otherre clutch his shirt with one hand, saw him draw the free fist back, and was unable to do anything. The blow blotted out sight but brought back sense. In agony he found the will to move and twisted aside from the next blow. Otherre's fist went into the mahogany, and the man cried out hoarsely.

Hogarth's shirt tore in the man's fist as he tried to twist out from beneath Otherre's grasp and the bar. He brought his knee into Otherre's groin and knew a savage satisfaction at the groan of utter pain this blow brought. But Otherre bellied up against him, refusing to let him get away. Hogarth's next spasmodic attempt to free himself carried them into Rane, and his feet tangled in Rane's legs. He went down with the dazed, stubborn Otherre falling heavily on top of him.

Then, lying twisted beneath the man, Hogarth heard a crashing sound and past Otherre's shoulder saw that Are had leaped through the window, glass and all, unable to contain himself any longer. He was charging toward them with the frame torn completely out of the wall and dangling around his bloody neck, the shotgun forgotten in one hand. From the other side the floor shuddered to Sigrod's feet. In a terrible spasm Hogarth tried to writhe from beneath Otherre's oppressive weight. The man stubbornly held him down, gathering the strength to strike again.

Oh, God, thought Hogarth, *here it comes,* and then both Sigrod and Are were in on it, rocking the room with their hoarse Viking bellows.

"Siger, siger, siger. . . !"

It gave him the sense of being in the middle of a pack of frenzied beasts. He made one last violent effort to free himself, heaving up beneath Otherre and battering a fist again and again into the man's face. Then he sank down beneath a wave of kicks and blows. Sight spun into a vortex of pain. Otherre's broken knuckles smashed him in the face. Sigrod's boot crushed in his ribs. Are's clawing hands gouged at his mouth. The agony whirled him faster and faster down that funnel toward the black abyss at the bottom. *Damn you, Kerry,* he thought, *if you didn't get her away!* — and then it was all gone.

Chapter Twelve

It was quiet when he regained consciousness. From somewhere far off he heard the drumming croak of sage hens. He was warm and drowsy and did not feel the pain at first. Then it came, throbbing through his body. When he tried to move, it stabbed at him.

He stopped moving and opened his eyes. He was in a bed, a tester bed with worn damask hangings. There were chairs in the room, upholstered in blue leather, studded with brass nails — shabby leather and tarnished nails. The rug looked like a Brussels carpet, handsome once, worn thin now.

His right hand hurt, and he took it from beneath the cover, wincing with pain that each movement brought, and saw that it was splinted and bandaged. His face felt raw, and he felt the cotton and plaster of bandages across his cheek and forehead.

He lay there, trying to imagine where he could be. The room made him think of Kerry's house with its memories of past magnificence. Then he heard footsteps in the hallway outside, and a door was opened.

Kerry Arnold came in. She was wearing the watered silk dress. It made the flesh of her neck and arms look like cream in the dusk of the room. She came over and sat on the bed beside him. Her eyes were softer than he had ever seen them before. She put her hand on his shoulder, and there was a husky compassion in her voice.

"Bob?"

He felt the flesh of his lips crack as he moved them to speak. "Wastewin?"

Kerry shook her head. "The girl got away." She put her fingers against his mouth, cool and soothing, as he started to protest. "I couldn't help it, Bob. It was either you or her. Do you think I could ride away from there with them beating you like that? I had to shame the men of the town into stopping it. The Trygvessons weren't even going to quit once you were unconscious." A subdued horror washed over her face. "They were like wild animals, Bob, like beasts."

"And you thought Wastewin would be safe with them." Hogarth settled defeatedly against the bed. "How did she escape?"

"I told Kidder to watch her while I ran across the street. There was a big crowd around the saloon doors, but they wouldn't make a move till it was obvious that you were completely through. Doc Powdre got hold of Are's shotgun and beat the Trygvessons off with it. While I was gone, Kidder said the woman tripped him up and got past him to one of those horses Jigger brought down from the stable. Jigger mounted up and tried to catch her. He said he never saw such a rider."

"I know what he meant." Hogarth was silent for a moment, staring beyond her. Then he said: "I don't remember being brought here."

"You started to regain consciousness in Doc Powdre's office. He knew you'd be in a lot of pain, so he gave you a sedative."

"What's the damage?" he asked.

"Right hand broken, six ribs broken, bruises from the bottom of your feet to the top of your head." She shook her head compassionately. "Doc Powdre says it will take a long time in bed before you can go anywhere."

"Who's going anywhere?"

She was studying him closely. "Most men would . . . after a beating like that. The town takes it for granted you'll leave now."

"Then they take too much for granted."

He saw a shine come into her eyes. "Bob," she whispered. There was a flush to her cheeks, a triumph in the way her chin lifted. She swayed forward, and for a moment he thought she was going to come into his arms. Then her eyes dropped to his side, and she checked herself. He knew what she was thinking. His ribs were broken.

"I wish I could hold you . . . tight." Her voice was soft, low.

He tried to grin, felt his lips crack again. "You can."

She shook her head, smoothing the covers gently across his chest. "You've got to rest, Bob. You've got to get well."

He was sicker than he realized those first few days. The doctor came again, gave him more sedatives. He slept most of the time. Kerry told him Waco had come to see him that first day, but he was not awake. Waco came again the third day, and Kerry ushered him in. Hogarth could not help noticing how stiff and reserved the man was in her presence. Perhaps she sensed it, too. She soon left them alone.

Waco held his scuffed Stetson in both hands, twisting the brim. "I wish to hell I'd been there, Bobby. I just wish to hell I'd been there."

Hogarth smiled at him. "Thanks, Waco. We could have taken 'em."

The man sat on a chair, still looking awkward, and pulled out his makings. He rolled a cigarette for Hogarth, stuck it in his mouth, lit it. Hogarth took a grateful drag.

"Thanks," he said. "I been hungry for that."

Waco was rolling one for himself. "When will you be well enough to go?"

131

"Would you let a beating scare you out?"

Waco leaned toward him. "It ain't that, Bobby. Hell, I know you ain't scared off by that. It's just that rotten grass again. Can't you see it now? That wasn't just an ordinary beating them Trygvessons gave you. They were crazy. They were taking something out on you that had been building up for years."

"What?"

"I don't know. That's just it. Part of it was that Indian gal, I guess. Part of it was that deal you pulled with the cattle. But that wasn't all. There was something else, something more. And it must be something pretty ugly to turn men that crazy. This basin is tainted, Bobby."

"You're talking like an old woman."

Waco sat up straight in his chair. His face looked tight and raw. His eyes were squinted almost shut.

Kerry tapped on the partly opened door then stepped in with two bottles of beer. There was a smile on her face, but it faded as she saw how stiffly Waco sat.

"I'd thought you'd like a drink," she said.

Waco stood up, getting his hat. "Not for me, thanks. I best be trailing."

Hogarth lifted one of his bandaged hands. "Waco. . . ?"

"Never mind, Bobby," Waco said. "Some men got to be hit over the head before they see something. I thought maybe you'd been hit enough."

He walked out, spurs clattering and jingling down the long hall. Kerry put the beers down. She did not seem surprised.

"I couldn't help overhearing part of that," she said. "What does he think is tainting the basin?"

Hogarth said: "Waco gets feelings like that. Sometimes they're right. Sometimes they're wrong."

132

"What do you think this time?"

He moved his head irritably. "The Trygvessons are primitive men. I saw nothing more in it than a bunch of animals venting their rage on someone they hate." She sat down. There was a look of relief on her face, and it made him ask: "Why? Don't tell me you think there's something in what Waco says?"

She shook her head. "I don't know. I just thought you might have heard something."

"Heard something?"

"From the Trygvessons, I mean." She turned to him, laying a hand gently on his arm. "You're bound to, sooner or later, Bob. I tried to make my peace with the Trygvessons a long time ago. I thought they were decent people . . . basically. They're honest and God-fearing and the hardest-working men in the basin. They don't often go into these rages." She shook her head, frowning at the floor. "But I've always had the feeling that they never quite got over the bitterness that stood between them and my father."

"But surely you've proved to them. . . ."

"That's it. Have I? They balk at so many of the things I suggest. I don't think they will ever trust me completely. It goes even deeper than that. They hated my father bitterly, Bob. I think some of it still remains."

He stirred restlessly in the bed. "Don't you think part of it is this rustling? It's making everybody jumpy and suspicious. If we could get that out of the way, it would clear the air."

"Maybe you're right," she said doubtfully.

Chapter Thirteen

The days following were the hardest. For a man used to activity and movement, staying in bed was torture. But worse than that was the torture of having Kerry so near and yet so far. She played endless card games with him. And she always won, because he could not concentrate on the games. His days seemed filled with the sight and sound and smell of her, so poignantly desirable to him that his feelings approached pain.

Sometimes he thought she deliberately tantalized him, wearing dresses that accented every curve of her magnificent body, letting her hip touch him when she sat on the bed, giving him those cool good night kisses, full of so much promise and stopping before any of the promise could be fulfilled. But he was too weak to do anything about it.

Finally he was able to sit up. His ribs were healing well, and Doc Powdre at last took the splint off his right hand. Calf time was coming and spring roundup. Kerry could not spend so much time with him. She was out on the range, down where Joe Hide and Morry Lucas were branding her share of Cramer's cattle. And when spring roundup started, Morry or Joe would come up to the big house almost every night, after Hogarth's lights were out, to go over the tally books with Kerry. Hearing the murmur of their voices in the kitchen downstairs, acutely conscious of all Kerry's comings and goings, Hogarth did not think he could stand the confinement much longer.

It was against the doctor's orders but, when Kerry was

gone, Hogarth began getting up and moving around the room. At first he was sick and dizzy. But soon he overcame that, and he could walk about for longer periods. And one night his immense restlessness got the better of him. He heard a horse snort out front, and in a moment the voices began in the kitchen. It would be Morry or Joe. He wanted to talk to a man again, to smell the dust and the sweat and the grass on him, to see the sunburn on his face. He put on his Levi's and boots and a robe Kerry had given him and started downstairs. The voices seemed to be rising and falling, almost in anger. He heard a man's voice, husky, bitter. Then, as he reached the bottom of the stairs and turned into the hall that led into the kitchen, he heard Kerry say: "But was it on the barefoot horse, Dagget? That's the whole point. Was it on the barefoot horse?"

Hogarth had reached the kitchen door before she spoke the name. He checked himself there as she finished, staring at the man who stood by the kitchen table. Lee Dagget was dressed in his shaggy bearskin coat and greasy rawhide leggins. There was no bandage on his face now, and the healed scar made a chalky track across the sharp edge of his cheekbone and into the gaunt hollow beneath. The light seemed to blaze up in his foxy eyes with his first sight of Hogarth. Kerry wheeled to see what he was looking at.

"Bob," she said sharply. "What are you doing down here?"

Hogarth moved on into the kitchen, his gaze still fixed on Dagget. "Having trouble, Kerry?"

"Of course not." She stopped, as if realizing suddenly what the full implications of this meeting were. She glanced back to Dagget then said: "Don't be a couple of fools now. That's all over. I won't have it in my house."

"What's that about a barefoot horse?" Hogarth asked.

Kerry looked back at him with a sharp shift of her head. She was frowning, her lips compressed. At her obvious hesitation he said: "You still don't trust me."

She bit her lip. She glanced again at Dagget. "It isn't that," she said. A malicious smile was growing on Dagget's mouth, and he started to say something. Kerry cut him off with her own words. "It's as I told you before, Bob. It's just a crazy business. It's got us all jumpy. Dagget came to tell me he found those barefoot tracks on my land east of Medicine Wheel Creek."

"What were you doing there?" Hogarth asked him.

Dagget's lips parted, but again Kerry cut him off. "As a matter of fact I'd sent Morry into Meeteetse today to leave word that I wanted to see Dagget. I need help. Joe and Morry can't handle the spring roundup and brand Cramer's cows, too." She saw the bleak expression enter Hogarth's face and made a disgusted sound. "Now don't be like that. Dagget is the only decent man I can get. He rode for Dad a long time, and he's ridden for me. Despite your trouble with him, he's a hard worker, Bob, and he's straight. After all, your trouble really wasn't with him. He was just doing what Chapel paid him to do."

"I never saw an ordinary cowhand wear his gun up under his arm that way," Hogarth said.

"And I never knew an ordinary cowhand who fanned a gun when he shot it, the way they say you did with Templeton." Her cheeks were flushed and her eyes were glittering brightly. "Now this has gone far enough. I need Dagget's help, Bob, and I'm not going to let a foolish grudge make me late to roundup. Promise me you'll both stop acting like children."

Before either of them could speak, there was a knock on the back door. Kerry walked over to open it and admit Joe

Hide. He looked at all of them with a grin, holding the tally books in his hand.

"Big tally today, Kerry. Thought you might like to check it."

"Can't it wait, Joe?"

"There are a couple of things I'd like to find out. That man from Tincup was over again today, claims some of his steers are still mixed in with our Lodgepole Creek bunch."

"All right," she said impatiently. She looked at Hogarth. "Can I leave you alone a moment?"

Hogarth looked at Dagget. The man touched his scar then smiled maliciously. "Everything will be all right," he said.

She studied the man with narrow eyes finally asking: "Will it?"

His eyes met hers, and his grin faded. "I told you," he said. "Everything will be all right."

"Very well." She inclined her head toward the stove. "Perhaps some coffee after your long ride?"

She and Hide disappeared down the hall, going to the office at the front of the house. Dagget moved to the stove, spurs clattering softly. He lit the fire and moved the coffee pot over it.

"Got a quirly?"

"My makings are upstairs," Hogarth said.

"So you got her," Dagget said.

Hogarth felt surprise and then anger ran thinly through him. He walked to the table and sat down. "Does it look that way?" he asked.

Dagget turned toward him. He was smiling again, that malicious smile, and it did not relieve the wolfish hostility in his face.

"You *think* you got her," he said. "But it's really the other way around. She's got you. I know how she works, Hogarth.

I been in this basin since her pappy owned it. You'd like to know some of the things I've seen."

"Hold it, Dagget," Hogarth said. He was leaning across the table. There was a silvery color to his eyes, and anger made his face gaunt. "Don't come to me with any dirty bunkroom talk. I won't listen to it."

Dagget's smile faded. "Yes, you will," he said. "Because there's a lot of things you don't understand in this basin, Hogarth, and you'd like to find out mighty bad. I'll tell you one of them. You'll never get Kerry. No more than George Chapel or Charles Tremaine or Rane or Otherre could get her." He laughed huskily. "Does that surprise you? It shouldn't. There ain't a man in this basin who hasn't wanted her, Hogarth. And who's got her? Not a one of them. She's used 'em all. She's led 'em on. She's wrapped 'em around her little finger. She's got what she wanted out of them, and then she's dropped 'em."

Hogarth came sharply to his feet, almost upsetting the chair. "Dagget. . . !"

"Don't be a fool." The man walked to the table, facing Hogarth across it. The stink of his ancient bearskin coat hung so rancidly in the room it almost gagged Hogarth. "I know how weak you are. I could knock you over with my finger. But I don't have to. I don't have to pay you back for this scar. I don't even have to tell you what I know. You'll find it all out for yourself. I'll get more pleasure out of watching you do that than I would out of whipping you right now."

Hogarth was trembling with his own anger and his sense of impotence. He realized how right the man was about his weakness. He would be a fool to lose control of himself. But something more than that held him from any reaction, something in Dagget's face. A frustrated hate, lying just beneath that insolence, gave his features a strained vindictiveness. It provided Hogarth with an answer to the whole thing.

"You say *every* man in the valley," he told Dagget. "Couldn't you have her either, Lee?"

The man's eyes almost shut. His face looked like he had been brutally whipped. For a moment Hogarth thought Dagget would hit him. But he didn't. He settled back on his heels. He reached up to run his fingers across the scar.

"Maybe," he said, "I will pay you for this, after all."

Chapter Fourteen

He slept poorly that night, knowing Dagget was in the bunkhouse. He rose early and dressed completely and went down to the kitchen. Even Ching was not up yet, and Hogarth warmed over the coffee and had a cup, bitter and black. The sun was up, streaming brilliantly into the kitchen, and he opened the door to let the spring scent of poplars come in. He took the coffee pot and two cups into the living room in time to meet Kerry coming downstairs.

She always wore some dark hue to accent the intense whiteness of her skin. Green, this time, a light summer dress that clung like a caress to the proud shape of her breasts and the long curve of her legs. She stopped in the doorway, an indulgent smile on her lips, frankly allowing him to admire. Then, with a chuckle, she moved over to pour herself a cup of coffee.

"I think you're a lecher," she said.

"You'd make any man a lecher."

She stood by the mantel, watching him from eyes still heavy-lidded with sleep. Her hair was perfectly groomed. "I hope you settled your differences with Dagget."

"I don't think we'll ever do that. The stripe will always be on his face."

She put the cup on the mantel, walking toward him. "I thought it was over between you two," she said. "I thought what happened was past. I thought you were grown-up men, not a couple of kids." She was before him, her arms slipping about his neck, her lips pouting. "And I do need him, Hogarth."

It was not what she said, but the way she said it, whispering, her sea-green eyes almost hidden behind slumberous lids — and her face three inches away. It was the first real kiss they'd had since the beating. It was the first time she could release her hunger, her passion, without causing him agony. Even so, it hurt. Her body was pressed so hard against his that it sent pain in sharp little jumps across his healing ribs, through the bruised nerves of his chest and legs and arms. Pain mingled with his own passion and was lost in it. Her arms were locked behind his back. Then she began fighting to get free. But it had gone too far this time. His voice was husky and broken.

"Kerry. . . ."

"No, Bob. Please."

He fought to hold her. "Kerry, you can't go on teasing like this. You can't go on using your body like this to get what you want. You can't expect a man to take it forever."

"Bob, stop it, stop it!"

She finally twisted free, her breasts heaving. She wheeled and walked to the mantel, her back to him. Her breathing made a sobbing sound in the room.

"Who's teasing who?" she asked bitterly. "Do you think I'm made of ice?"

"I can't apologize," he said. "You're not a little girl. You should know what happens."

"I don't ask you to apologize. But don't ask me to, either. Maybe I want it as bad as you do, Hogarth. But next time I want it decently, that's all."

He moved over behind her, still trembling, not knowing whether it was all weakness or all desire. "Of course you do," he said. "It's my fault in a way, Kerry, for letting it go

141

so long like this. But it digs back into my life. I've told you before. I was just a ramrod. I nearly killed myself to get that job because I thought it was what a woman wanted. But it wasn't enough. She said no. My whole life changed right there. It was something that had been building for a long time, but that was the turning point. I swore by heaven and earth that the next time I asked a woman to marry me, I'd have more than seventy-five a month and a saddle."

She had not faced him yet. But her face was gradually turning, so that her profile was coming into view. "It wouldn't matter what you had, Bob, to the right woman."

"It would matter to me. And now I've got it, Kerry. Those Cramer cattle will set us all up. I'm my own boss. I own as much land and as much cattle as anybody in this basin. It's time we quit torturing ourselves. Will you marry me, Kerry?"

She turned to him. Her breasts were lifted high. There was a glittering look to her eyes, and her teeth gleamed through parted lips, giving her face a sort of savage eagerness.

"Bob," she whispered. "Bob. . . ."

Before she could finish, there was the stutter of hoofs on the hard earth outside. Leather squeezed as someone swung off a snorting, blowing horse by the porch, and then boots clattered across the planking. The knock jarred Hogarth. He felt a sharp anger at the intruder as Kerry pulled reluctantly free. She petted her hair into place as she went to the door. It was Oswald Karnes, bursting in as she opened the door, sweat dripping off his face. His little eyes were wide and shining, and he was wheezing so heavily he could hardly speak.

"Kerry . . . ran my horse all the way . . . never such a ride! Something bad! Tremaine. He's been killed!"

Hogarth could not see the expression on Kerry's face. Her back was to him. She stared at Karnes without speaking. The fat lawyer stared back. Finally, sucking in another huge breath, he asked: "Did you hear me, Kerry? I. . . !"

"I heard you," she said. Her voice was low, strained. She shook her head helplessly from side to side. "How . . . how did it happen?"

Karnes staggered to a chair, lowering his rotund body into it. "Got to sit down. Exhausted. Never had such a. . . ." He pulled a handkerchief out, mopping at his shining brow. Sweat lay like grease in the folds of his face. "Kasna came in this morning with the news. Someone shot Charlie last night . . . in his home." He shuddered then added: "In the back of his head. He was murdered!"

Hogarth turned and walked to the window. The mountains were visible from here, black and shaggy against the morning sky. He felt sick at his stomach. He had liked Charles Tremaine.

Karnes was not breathing so heavily now. He glanced at Hogarth, that circumspect, bird-like glance. "There's going to be an inquest. Are was in town, and he's already ridden to his father with the news. Chapel will hear soon enough. The cooperative will be meeting today. We have a problem on our hands."

Chapter Fifteen

Meeteetse stirred with a subdued excitement, hitch racks lined with cow ponies from the various outfits represented by the board. The four white Trygvesson stallions filled the rack before the Big Horn Building, three of the Tee Broom horses from Chapel's outfit across the street in front of the saloon. Chapel and Templeton drew in beside these, while Kerry drove her spring buggy into Gilroy's Livery next door to the Bullhorn Saloon.

She helped Hogarth out and, as Gilroy led the matched team back toward the other end, they had a moment alone in the cool silence.

"This is a chance, if you want it," she said, clutching Hogarth's arm. "You stacked it up so Karnes will back you, didn't you?"

"I think we can count on him," said Hogarth.

"The Trygvessons have one voice, and Chapel one," she said. "That makes two to our three. I don't know why they called the meeting. Whether they mean to elect a new president in Charlie's place this time or not, I'll jump the gun and nominate you."

"Coming?" queried George Chapel, appearing in the doorway.

They followed him across the street and into the Big Horn Building. The first thing Hogarth saw, entering the offices of the cooperative, were the Trygvessons, standing together against the wall. Are and Otherre stood on either side of Rane in a close, protective way, and Hogarth could see the palpable tension fill their great bodies as he entered. Are's face flushed, and his tongue made a nervous flick across his lower lip. Otherre began rubbing those scarred, battered knuckles with one hand. Hogarth stopped just inside the door, waiting for them to speak. Suddenly Sigrod's rumble filled the room like the first muffled shattering of submerged icebergs.

"Say hello to Hogarth, Rane," said the grizzled father. "This is Hogarth. Surely you remember him? Say hello."

At first Hogarth thought Rane was staring at him. Then he realized there was no expression in the man's eyes. They were blank and childish. His head made a faint, dazed movement.

"*Vaer dig selv nok,*" he said mechanically.

"That is the motto of our house, Hogarth," said Sigrod, a sense of terrible, restrained savagery in his guttural voice. "It means, 'To yourself be sufficient.' A good motto, isn't it? A good motto for a boy to remember who can't remember anything else since some Texan kicked him in the head. Just sits there and stares into the fireplace as if he could see clear back to Sweden. And all he can say when we talk to him is this. Say it again, Rane, say it again for Hogarth."

"*Vaer dig selv nok,*" muttered Rane emptily.

"Yes, to yourself be sufficient." Sigrod's hands began to open and close, his voice started rising. "He's sufficient to himself, isn't he, Hogarth? He doesn't need anyone now. All he has to do is sit in front of the fireplace and. . . ."

"Sigrod, please," interrupted Oswald Karnes, waddling around from behind the long table. "You promised me." He turned deprecatingly to Hogarth. "Glad to see you're well enough to come in, Hogarth, though it's unfortunate it has to be for such a tragic reason. None of us can imagine who

145

would want to kill Tremaine. He was so well liked around here. Ah, well, shall we call the meeting to order?"

"May I suggest your sons go outside, Sigrod," said Kerry. "You're the only proper representative of your family at this meeting."

"They have a right to hear everything that's said," muttered Sigrod thickly.

"I think Kerry's right, Sigrod," Chapel told him in a stiff voice. "I left Templeton downstairs, and the rest of the outfits are satisfied with hearing the minutes read at the general assembly."

Sigrod growled something in Swedish, moving his great-thewed arm in a jerky gesture for the boys to leave. Otherre was still rubbing those battered knuckles as he passed. His eyes held a bleak hatred, meeting Hogarth's eyes for an instant. Chapel shut the door behind them.

"Now we can get down to business," said Karnes. "Yes! For a matter of convenience, may I make a move that we elect a president pro-tem, and suggest myself. . . ."

"Why pro-tem?" said Kerry. "We'll have to elect a regular officer sooner or later anyway. We're all here now. I nominate Bob Hogarth for president."

"Uh-uh-uh. . . ," stuttered Karnes, his puffy face lifting as if he had been slapped, but as he saw Chapel start to speak, his cunning mind grasped all the ramifications of this move, and he drowned whatever Chapel started to say with his own quick, chuckling recovery. "Of course, of course, well, Kerry, you're really riding a biscuit-cutter today, yes siree. I think that an admirable idea. I second the motion *and* the nomination. I think Hogarth has revealed singular capacity for such a position. I move we take a vote."

"Wait a minute. . . ," started Chapel.

146

"Second the motion," said Kerry.

"Hold it. . . !"

"All in favor of Hogarth, say aye," said Karnes, breaking in on Chapel.

"Now stop your horses!" shouted Chapel, standing up so abruptly he almost knocked his chair over. "You can't bull a thing like this through, Karnes."

Karnes's face held a wonderful innocence. "Who's bulling anything through, Chapel? We observed all the formalities, didn't we? Let's not get hot under the collar. It seems to me you're the only one trying to bull things through. Let's keep the meeting orderly. How about a vote on this. Mine is aye."

"Aye," said Kerry.

"No," said Chapel vehemently.

"No!" roared Trygvesson.

Karnes allowed his pudgy head to turn toward Hogarth, but Chapel started to rise again. "He can't vote for himself!"

"The President of the United States has the right to vote," said Karnes. "What are you trying to do, undermine democracy? Let's hear your word, Hogarth."

"Aye," said Hogarth.

"Then that settles it."

"That settles nothing," snapped Chapel, rising again. "Kasna is here as a representative of Tremaine. He has Tremaine's vote in this."

Apparently Kerry had not counted on this. Hogarth saw surprise shift across her face and then a certain, vague defeat. Kasna's wooden face turned toward Trygvesson. Watching the jet eyes, Hogarth saw what might have been taken for a vague rejection turn them dull. Then they shifted to Chapel, and brightened — with an antagonism Hogarth could not miss. Finally, they were on Hogarth.

147

"Tremaine always liked you," said Kasna and paused a moment. "Aye."

Sigrod jumped to his feet, chair spinning back to crash against the wall, his great fist thumping the table so hard it knocked off the papers Chapel had been taking minutes on. "I won't stay in a cooperative with him as president," he bellowed. "If you insist on this, I'm pulling out!"

"You can't," began Karnes, "your contract. . . ."

"To hell with the contract," shouted the man. "I'll tear it up. I'll tear it up right in your face, Karnes. If you put Hogarth in, I'm through!"

"Then I guess you're through," said Kerry quietly from where she sat. "By vote Hogarth is in already."

Hogarth saw the man's intent and tried to rise and kick the chair out from under him so it would not impede his draw, but those ribs were still stiff, and his bad leg buckled. He had to clutch at the table to keep from falling and saw he could never get to his iron in time. Then the door swung open and a lazy, dusty, Texas drawl halted Sigrod's hand with his gun half drawn.

"Pull that the rest of the way," said Waco Williams, "and I'll blow you clear back to Eric the Red!"

Chapter Sixteen

Summer came with the trumpeting of rutting bulls in the swampy bottomlands along the Big Horn, and the quack of ducks across the marshes, and the sweet, resinous scent of yellow-leaved poplars about the Big Dipper house. It was here Kerry and Hogarth had come, following their marriage.

Those first weeks with her were something out of a dream to Hogarth, a dream of softness and richness and beauty he had held as only a distant hope all of his life. For a time he lost sight of the plans they had been working on, forgot the precarious position he occupied in the cooperative.

It was Kerry who started prodding him, several weeks after their wedding, to start strengthening his hold on what he had obtained. Waco had been staying at the Rocker T, but the Saturday five weeks following the wedding Hogarth invited him over to the Big Dipper. Waco did not try to hide his pleasure at seeing Hogarth again when they met on the long stone porch.

"Things have been moving so fast since you've been out at the Rocker T. I never rightly got a chance to thank you for saving my life there in the basin office." Hogarth smiled at Waco and seated him in one of the cane chairs. "I'd never have gotten my iron free the way I was fumbling around. Sigrod would've blown my lamp out for good."

Waco's grin was embarrassed. "I'd just left the trail herd outside town when I heard there was a meeting called. Had a little fuss getting through the Trygvessons at the bottom of the stairs. Heard Sigrod bellering, figured something was popping."

Hogarth opened some beer, handed a bottle to Waco. "How would you like to rod the Big Bit for the cooperative until we decide what is to be done with it, Waco? Tremaine had no heirs, and it needs a manager. Kasna just can't seem to handle it alone."

"Which would give you, in effect, control over three outfits . . . your Rocker T, Kerry's Big Dipper, and the Big Bit," said Waco.

"Someone has to be appointed," said Hogarth.

"Do your plans for the Big Bit extend beyond that?" asked the man.

Hogarth pursed his lips, staring into the distance behind Waco. Before he could answer, Kerry spoke from behind them. "Why not tell him, Bob?"

He had not been aware of her and twisted in his chair. "Tell him what, Kerry?"

She came around and took the third chair, smiling at Waco. "Tell him what's been on your mind concerning the Big Bit."

"What has been on my mind?"

Her smile turned indulgent. "Don't you ever get tired of his eternal reticence, Waco? You've divided that trail herd from Cheyenne among all the members of the cooperative by now, haven't you, Waco? I see you and Shorthorse Simms have already finished branding the Rocker T on the five hundred head Bob got. We've almost finished stamping my Big Dipper on, too. But one of Kasna's little inefficiencies has been failing to put the Big Bit on yet. The five hundred head allotted to Tremaine are still running around with nothing but that Texas road brand on them."

She paused a moment, studying Waco's face. "It's about

time to build the fall herd for the Indian agencies," she continued. "It will leave us all in a weakened position again, without enough brood stock to give us a safe margin for next year. That trail herd didn't give any one of us quite enough for that margin. But if we could contrive it, say, that one outfit would not have to contribute its full quota to the herd for the agency, that outfit would be left in an eminently favorable position for next year, a position strengthened even more by the contrasting weakness of the other outfits."

"You mean fill up the Rocker T and Big Dipper quotas with those cattle from the Big Bit?" said Hogarth.

"Isn't that what was in your mind, Bob?" she asked.

"Don't put words in my mouth," he said.

Something almost surprised crossed her face, and then a frigidity entered her voice. "I'm not putting anything in your mouth, or your mind, Bob. Don't try to tell me you haven't figured the possibilities. With only the road brand on those beeves allotted to the Big Bit, any brand can be put on for the government herd. We could make up the Big Bit's allotment out of Tremaine's original stock, with the Big Bit brand already on them. Then we could put the Rocker T on two hundred and fifty of those road-branded steers from Cheyenne, and the Big Dipper on the other two hundred and fifty."

"All of which would bleed the Big Bit dry and be the closest thing to a sticky loop I ever heard," said Waco, rising to his feet.

"Not at all!" bridled the woman. "That would leave the Rocker T and the Big Dipper enough brood stock for a substantial increase through the winter. With that increase we could replace what came from the Big Bit, next spring."

"You're rationalizing a bum deal, Kerry," Hogarth told her.

151

She flushed. "I don't see how you can say that with the kind of deal you just pulled off, buying cattle in Cheyenne with a check that didn't have any money behind it. Who was rationalizing then, calling it speculation? This sudden nobility is almost funny in the man who invited Oswald Karnes up here this afternoon to look for some loopholes in the cooperative's charter whereby he might gain control of even more land. What's the matter, are you getting slow on your feet, Bob? Are you afraid they'd find out? It wouldn't be any different than that other deal, except that the government money came through in time to cover the check to Moffet."

"No." Waco shook his head, started toward the steps. "Whether they find out or not, Kerry, doesn't matter. I just can't see it. I'd rather not be included."

"I thought you were Bob Hogarth's man," said Kerry, rising.

Waco turned slowly, and there was something in the detached study of his gaze on Kerry that disturbed Hogarth. "He always let me make my own decisions," said Waco.

"Your position has changed somewhat, Waco," said Kerry. "I think you must have seen that. The way things are stacked up now, either you are Bob's man or you're not. Maybe you'd better reconsider."

Waco did not speak. He stared at Kerry a moment longer, the weather lines of his angular face relaxing. He let his eyes move unhurriedly to Hogarth. They were blank and empty. Then he turned and went down the steps.

Hogarth held out an arm, starting after him. "Waco. . . ?"

"Bob!" The cutting tone of Kerry's voice stopped him. She put a hand on his arm. "I think he's made his choice, don't you?"

Hogarth stared into her narrowed eyes, trying to define

the strange emotion gathering in him. The delicate refinement of her face suddenly seemed to take on a cold calculation.

"Karnes can get you a man," she said. "You'd better do it today if you want to get to those cattle before Kasna starts putting the Big Bit on them."

Some guttural inarticulation formed in Hogarth's taut throat, and he moved his hand in a vague gesture toward the receding figure of Waco, staring emptily at Kerry, not yet willing to accept her casual dismissal of what had happened. He did not even turn at the footsteps behind him.

"Afternoon, Kerry, Bob," said Oswald Karnes, puffing up onto the porch and dropping into a chair with a heavy sigh. "Hot day, isn't it? Saw your saddle mate going down the road, Hogarth. You made him foreman of the Big Bit yet?" He began fumbling with his briefcase. "I brought the charter and contracts so you could see what I figured out. Each member, of course, is restricted as to the amount of land he can own personally, but the big owners are still pulling the old switch on the government under the homestead law. When they can't file on it themselves, they have one of their hands take out papers on a quarter section they happen to covet, making the land in effect theirs. There is nothing to prevent, for instance, Shorthorse Simms's taking two sections over on that strip belonging to the cooperative next to your Rocker T. Then there's another stretch up. . . ."

"Yeah, yeah," said Hogarth dimly, moving across the porch. "Talk it over with Kerry, will you, Karnes? I don't feel like discussing business today."

Karnes's brow raised in surprise. "What's the matter, Hogarth?"

Hogarth did not answer, limping faintly down the front of the house toward the stables, but it kept echoing in his

153

mind with a hollow, brazen clangor. *What's the matter, Hogarth?* He clenched his teeth, wishing he knew. Then there was that strange sensation he now felt sometimes with Kerry, of something, he realized, that had lain dormant within him almost from the first. Looking at her face which seemed to have become sharp and acquisitive, hearing her voice turn cold, seeing the subtle, deceptive shift of her mental gears — he had suddenly felt as if he were seeing himself.

He was riding one of her Big Dipper horses now, a tall, blood bay with the fine-boned aristocracy Kerry preferred. He heard Whitney in the corral, but somehow he did not want Kerry's foreman to saddle up for him, even though it caused his ribs pain to heave the corus off its peg in the tack room and carry it to the stalls. With the rig on, he stepped aboard the bay and turned it down the road after Waco. He caught up with the man about half a mile from the house.

"Waco!" Hogarth called out toward him.

Waco halted his horse until Hogarth had pulled up alongside. Without preliminary, he started forward again and broke right in at Hogarth: "Got everything you want now, Bobby boy, haven't you? President of the Big Horn Cooperative, living in a palace, married to the most beautiful woman in Wyoming, they say, controlling three of the best spreads in the association, money, position, cattle and more cattle!"

"Stow it in your yannigan bag, will you, Waco?" said Hogarth bitterly. "I don't want to leave it this way. You don't have to go along with that plan concerning the Big Bit beef."

"Noble of you," said Waco.

"No." Hogarth's voice held a dim anguish. "Cut it out, will

you? I know we haven't seen each other this last month or so, and it might look like Kerry's come between us some, but that isn't the truth. It's just the first few weeks after the wedding . . . you understand . . . and we'll soon be back on the old basis. You know I'm not going to use the Big Bit cattle that way . . . no matter what Kerry suggested."

"On the contrary," said Waco, "I think you are. Whether it was in your mind at first or not, she put it there. And whether you mean to or not, you end up agreeing with her, Bobby. You thought it was your trick when you first persuaded her to clinch that deal with Chapel, but look at it again. That's a woman's way, Hogarth, to make a man think it was him who figured out all the angles. I think maybe she's figuring two for your one. But there were a couple of things I didn't realize until recently, and the biggest one is how alike you two are! In a way Kerry Arnold's the perfect partner for you. I was wrong to have been against her and you together. You both want the same things. If there's any difference, it might be how you plan to go about getting the job done. But the ambition is there in both of you."

A sharp muscular twitch caught at Hogarth's cheek, and he was staring at Waco. "You do resent her, don't you?"

"I won't deny that," said Waco. "In fact, I just admitted it and admitted I was wrong, and that's why I'm pulling out, Bobby. Kerry was pretty close to the truth. I'm either your man or I'm not. Well, I want to get away before we take the next step, before it's too late."

Hogarth's voice was very quiet. "Just what would that mean?"

"What happened to Charlie Tremaine," said Waco.

"You'll have to do more explaining than that!"

"He was found shot to death in his own house," Waco replied. "Everyone knew he felt friendly toward you. Did he

155

buck, too, when you tried to get him to rope a bum steer?"
The blood drained from Hogarth's face but, before he could
answer, Waco fixed his eyes on him, meeting his gaze
frankly. "We always showed each other what was in our
pokes, Bobby boy. That's what's in mine. Ever get back to
San Antonio, look me up."

They had reached a creek, and he turned the dun to slide
it down the sandy bank into the shallows. Hogarth stared
blankly after the man. The water gurgled dimly about the
fetlocks of the dun. Waco's husky monotone rose above the
sound of the creek.

> *But one day he met a man a whole lot badder,*
> *And now he's dead. . . .*

The stunning detonation of the gunshot struck Hogarth's
consciousness, pulling him up so hard in the saddle that
the corresponding jerk of his hands on the reins caused the
bay to rear. The animal wheeled the other way before he
could pull it down. He had his gun out, firing at the blurred,
moving shape in the poplars farther up the bank of the
stream. Then the frenzied bay had wheeled back with its
head toward the stream, and Hogarth could see Waco. The
water still made that soft, gurgling sound about the man's
long body, stretched on its back in the shallows.

Hogarth swung off the bay and ran down the crumbling
bank into the water, dropping to his knees beside Waco.
The blood was coming from a hole in the man's narrow chest
and turning to a rusty murk in the water flowing down-
stream. Hogarth slipped an arm beneath Waco's head. The
movement opened Waco's eyes in a feeble, stuttering way.
They settled on the smoking gun in Hogarth's other hand.
Hogarth realized only then that he was still gripping the

weapon, and his gaze swung to it for a horrified instant, then back to Waco's eyes.

"No, Waco, no. . . !"

"I get in your way, Bobby boy?" mumbled the Texan. He tried to laugh and choked on it. "Guess I didn't hit the trail quite soon enough. Can't say I blame you, though. Man needs to hold onto what he has. And you have so much now, Bobby boy, everything you ever wanted. But I wouldn't have got in your way. I wouldn't have screwed you up. I just meant to ride on out and let you do whatever you wanted, Bobby . . . bad, good, or indifferent. . . ." A glazed look entered his eyes as he trailed off. He made an effort to focus them again. They rolled upward. A choking laugh shook him, the words coming out in a strangled prolation.

And now he's dead, and we're none the sadder. . . .

Chapter Seventeen

The sleek hairless hide of the bay gleamed like wet blood in the saturation of sweat drawn from it by the summer heat and the hard climb. The rarified atmosphere caused its delicate nostrils to flutter with the constant suction of its labored breathing. At a halt the slender legs trembled beneath the animal like quaking aspens. *I wish to hell I had that skewbald,* Hogarth thought, and then stifled it — because he would always associate Waco Williams with that pony, somehow, and Waco's death was only a week behind him. He still knew a dull, throbbing pain whenever he thought of it, and he thought of it often.

He drew a heavy breath, bending in the saddle to peer at the tracks he had been following from the Big Bit. They were of the inevitable barefoot horse, driving a couple of dozen steers from Tremaine's old outfit straight east across the river into the Big Horns. Medicine Peak thrust its shaggy head into a pale sky ahead of him. Brown needles carpeted the earth beneath the conifers, and heat clutched the silent stands of timber in its stifling fist. He had trouble getting the bay on up the slope. The strange tension was beginning to find its way through his other emotions now. He found his head cocked stiffly to one side and straightened it with a snap. But in another moment it was down again, listening for that weird chant.

Nothing came, however, as he climbed on toward the crest. He lacerated himself bitterly. *Why should she be there again? That was too much to expect. And why should he expect it? A dirty, stinking Indian squaw.* He tried to drive this vindictiveness from his mind, but it would not leave. He knew part of its cause. The quarrels between him and Kerry had become increasingly violent this last week. She had opposed his tracking this new rustling, and he had left the house in anger, knowing a new sense of freedom once he was in the saddle.

Now he could see the park five hundred feet below. The grass made a bright green splash against the darker hues of shaggy timber on every side. The cattle began drifting into sight near noon, cropping idly, some of them bedded down in the hot sun to chew their cuds. Hogarth was out of his Mackinaw and settled down against the warm rocks.

The water and the rich graze and the lazy sun held the cattle in the meadow all that day. They bedded down that night near the creek, and there was a moon to light the meadow for Hogarth. When it sank and the pitch-blackness before dawn blotted out all below him, Hogarth moved on downslope. He waited near the bottom, listening to the grunts and soft groans of the peaceful cattle. At dawn he moved back atop the ridge.

They drifted that day, higher into the mountains, and he followed, clinging to the cover of timberline pine. Again the cattle stopped in another jade-grassed park, and again he nested in the sun-warmed rocks of a ridge, watching, waiting. The light ran out, and night came, bringing its chill. He had drunk all his cold coffee and eaten most of his biscuits now. He had to keep moving around to stay awake. He was beginning to know discouragement. Maybe he was a fool. Maybe this wouldn't work at all.

It was the stubborn streak in him that made him stick. Another night and another day and he was growing as restless and spooky as his horse from the vigil. He finished the last of his venison the fifth evening. That filled him with a nagging sense of impending failure, and he faced the night in a depressed mood.

A full moon began to rise. The trees were skeletal silhouettes against its yellow orb. He could see the steers now, dark patches against the moon-silvered meadow. And one began to bawl. It was a new sound, different from the peaceful lowing to which he had become so accustomed. He rose, tightening the nose band so his horse could not whinny. Then he led it down through the scrub timber, through the juniper, dropping down to the edge of the meadow. There was definite movement among the cattle. He could make out two shadowy shapes, one larger than the other. A horse and rider, cutting a steer out of the herd.

Hogarth mounted the bay while watching the vague shapes move across the meadow toward its upper end. He paralleled the direction, moving gradually back to the height of the ridge. The meadow became a cañon, the cañon finally divided into three forks, and its sides became cliffs too steep for his horse to climb. He had to drop down into the bottom to follow the rider and the single steer. Part of the time he kept up by trailing; the moonlight was bright enough for him to see the tracks in the sand and loamy earth. The rest of the time, when he could do it without danger of being seen, he kept the rider in sight.

After an hour of tracing the winding cañon back into the Big Horns, a trail lifted them out of its depths and into the steep watersheds of the main mountains. The moon was sinking when the bold peak came into sight ahead. They passed above the Medicine Wheel, with its buffalo skull gleaming translucently in the fading light.

While there was still moonlight, he dropped down closer. And when the moon vanished and the utter darkness before

160

dawn closed in, he was near enough so that he did not lose his quarry.

It was a tense journey now. The snow was in close proximity, banked on unseen summits above, pressing its chill against Hogarth like a palpable weight. He was shivering despite the heavy Mackinaw, and his hands were stiff and numb. As the milky light of dawn streaked the sky, he saw the mountains massed on every side, black timbered, ancient. He took to the trees to avoid discovery. He could see the horse ahead now. A pinto. And the rider. Wastewin.

It came as no surprise. She was muffled to the ears in a hoary old buffalo coat. It reached her knees and hid all but the jet-black top of her head and the dirty buckskin of her leggins. She was drooping in the saddle and free-bitting the pinto most of the time.

Hogarth's ears began to pop, and he realized that they were gradually losing altitude. The mountains began to spread away, and finally he followed her through a saddle in a ridge. He saw that ahead there were no more mountains, only a vast wasteland stretching as far as the eye could see, a plain of red sandstone into which time and erosion had carved a veritable labyrinth of twisted gorges and tortuous cañons. This, he knew, was the badlands. They'd come clear through the Big Horns and were on the eastern side of the mountains. Ahead, in the north-central part of the state, lay the headwaters of the Powder River and the Hole-in-the-Wall country. As Tremaine had said, Hole-in-the-Wall had always been a vague, half-mythical section. Few men knew where it actually lay. It was a legend that traveled far, for Hogarth had heard of it even in Texas — a valley guarded by the formidable escarpment of a red rock wall, two hundred feet high and thirty-five miles long, with only one entrance in the whole of its length, a cañon so narrow that a single man could prevent an army from getting through. Hogarth knew to what enormous exaggeration these legendary hideouts could grow. Yet, despite Tremaine's scoffing attitude, Hogarth couldn't put it out of his mind.

He lifted sharply in the stirrups as he realized how long he had held his horse there, gazing at the twisted land ahead — and realized what it had cost him. For Wastewin was no longer in sight ahead. He was about to boot his jaded animal down into the trees when he caught a shadowy motion in the lower timber. He held his horse on a tight rein till he caught a flash of that buffalo coat between two tree trunks.

He understood then what had happened. The woman had probably hobbled the steer and was coming to check her back trail. In another moment she would see him. He wheeled his horse and drove it up the steep slope of the saddle into dense scrub timber. Here he slowed down and let the animal pick its way through the twisted junipers and matted oaks till he was hidden from the saddle. He stopped and dismounted.

Wastewin appeared below. The ground was hard, and he had left but dim tracks. She wasn't looking for sign, anyway; her whole attention was upon the country through which they had already passed. She held her pinto at a stand-still, while from the saddle she scanned the valley below. Eventually, she went on, dropping down to the bottom of the valley and rising to another, higher crest, from which she could see even farther along her back trail. Hogarth did not follow, knowing she would be returning soon. He saw her silhouette skylighted on a higher ridge, half a mile away. She remained there for ten minutes before turning back, descending to the valley through the timber.

When she was half way down, Hogarth saw a new motion at the head of the valley. Dust rose in a fragile scarf to die against the sky. The motion then became riders, coming hard down the floor of the valley. He was higher than Wastewin now and realized that he could see the riders, although they were invisible to her. She kept moving down through the trees, toward the valley's bottom, apparently unaware of the approaching horsemen. He kicked the bay into motion, dropping off the crest and into the saddle, a keen apprehension running through him. Those riders wouldn't be coming so fast without purpose. Had they seen Wastewin skylighted against that ridge? Could it be Lieutenant Bannister and his troop?

With apprehension growing to fear, he put his horse into a run down the steep slope toward the valley. He could see the tawny flash of Wastewin's buffalo coat almost at the bottom now. He was half way down when he caught full sight of the riders. They were only a quarter of a mile away from the spot where Wastewin would emerge from the trees. There were two of them, riding white horses, the Trygvessons.

He kicked his horse into greater speed, taking the chance of sliding on the talus or plunging headlong into the densely packed trees. Dodging through lodgepoles and spruce, kicking up a spray of pine needles, ducking low branches, clawed by chokecherry, he continued crashing down the slope. As he ran from the fringe of timber into a park that leveled off and became the bottom of the valley, Wastewin emerged from the timber on the opposite slope.

She saw him plunge into the open and pulled her pinto to a startled halt. At the same time the two Trygvessons appeared around a shoulder of the mountain, riding full tilt into the lower end of the park. Hogarth saw Wastewin's head jerk toward them then back at him. Wildly, she pulled the pinto around and booted it back up the slope.

"Wastewin," he shouted. "They'll catch you that way. Don't run from me. Come back!"

But she was already in timber. He knew how worn down her horse was. It could never outdistance the Trygvessons uphill. He saw it stumble and fall as it lathered into a heavy run through the upslope timber. Half way across the park himself, driving his own stumbling horse mercilessly, he saw the Trygvessons turn into the trees after her. Their animals were obviously fresher and closed the gap quickly. He reached the edge of the park and entered the trees. The squealing of horses, the husky roar of their breathing and the clatter of their hoofs, made a bedlam in the timber. He saw Wastewin cross a meadow half way to the top, her horse weaving and tripping. A moment later Otherre appeared, driving his big white horse behind her. Then Are. He headed for the right flank, and Otherre cut around to wedge her off from the front. She pulled up, trying to wheel away, but Otherre ran his horse across in front of her.

Still in the trees Hogarth saw her stop, helplessly trapped between them. As this happened, Are immediately wheeled his horse back toward the lower edge of the park. He had that double-barreled shotgun out, and he lifted it to cover Hogarth as he charged out of the trees. Hogarth pulled his animal to a halt, staring down the twin muzzles of the lethal weapon.

"I'll use it this time, Hogarth," Are warned.

Hogarth's animal fiddled and groaned beneath him, sucking air like a bellows, the stench of its lather turning the air rank and sour. He could have pulled his gun long before, but he had known how useless that would be, with Wastewin right in the line of fire. Otherre had taken her bridle reins from her and was leading her down to Hogarth. She sat stiffly in the saddle, black eyes burning with fear and rage. Otherre pulled his great white horse to a halt, easing his ponderous weight back in the saddle. There was triumph in his glittering blue eyes, though he did not smile.

"Now," he said. "What are you doing here, Hogarth?"

Hogarth's belly felt empty with a growing defeat. "I might ask you the same," he replied.

Otherre folded his scarred hands across the saddle horn. "We have long known the rustler was taking cattle on east of here. But even when we found a trail in the mountains, we couldn't follow it beyond the edge of the badlands. Charles Tremaine's death convinced us even more that this thing had to be stopped, one way or another. We have been patrolling this eastern border of the mountain night and day since the meeting at Meeteetse. From his post on a peak north of here, Are saw her on this ridge above us. He picked me up where I was scouting the valley."

"We might have known you'd be in on the rustling," Are said.

"You're still jumping to conclusions," Hogarth told him. "I was following her."

"Where are the cattle?"

"There's only one steer," Hogarth said. "I think she hobbled it on the edge of the badlands."

"We'll see," Otherre said.

They made him drop his guns, and Otherre picked them up, lashing the saddle gun under his stirrup leather and stuffing the six-shooter in his saddlebag. Then, still leading Wastewin's horse, he headed across the valley. Are brought up the rear, shotgun still covering them. Hogarth pulled in beside Wastewin, but she stared straight ahead, refusing to look at him or to speak. They crossed the saddle and found the steer hobbled in the mouth of the cañon, where it opened into the badlands. It was so weary it had not moved six feet from where she had left it. Otherre frowned at the surrounding country.

"There must be more."

"Look at the sign," Hogarth told him.

Otherre got down and studied the prints a long time, shaking his head in a baffled way. "Just her pinto and this steer, Are."

"Take her to Father," Are said importantly. "He'll know what to do."

"I imagine he will," Hogarth said.

Otherre looked up sharply, anger mottling his cheeks. "We want none of your sarcasm. You will come with us, too."

Hogarth felt his defeat become a sickness in him. This was what he had fought against from the beginning. He tried to argue them out of it, but that lifelong subservience to their father made them deaf to his protests. Wastewin was too beaten down to object. Weariness lay like a stain beneath her high cheekbones and in the hollows of her black eyes. Her slim body was deeply bowed in the buffalo coat, and her buckskinned legs hung slack against the stirrup leathers of her saddle.

With Otherre leading again and Are bringing up the rear, they passed back into the mountains, heading northward. Though the Trygvessons actually ran their herd in the Big Horn Basin, grazing the cattle no farther east than Hogarth had his herd, their house was much deeper in the mountains. It lay at the headwaters of Medicine Wheel Creek, closer to the badlands than it was to the other side. They reached it in the afternoon, a sprawling log house with a steep roof and bottle windows, half hidden in a mass of cottonwoods. Hogarth saw that all their horses were not

166

these big, white animals. There was a pack pole corral at the rear of the house, filled with a dozen horses — bays and duns and roans — all smaller, tighter-coupled mounts, more suited to cattle work than the half-Percherons of which the Trygvessons seemed so fond.

As they approached the house, a half dozen huge hounds lunged off the porch and rushed out in a pack, making the afternoon hideous with their baying. They flooded around the riders, and Are had to shout angrily at them to keep the animals from jumping up on the horses. The door opened, and Sigrod stepped into view. He was dressed in a pair of buckskin leggins, black with grease, and a woolly sheepskin vest pulled over a thick red shirt. The strong sun turned his long white hair to a silvery mane that massed and coiled across his shoulders. He said nothing as they approached. He stood with his feet planted wide, the implacable mold of his face carving the seams deep as wounds about his eyes and mouth.

"Where did you find them?" he shouted.

Otherre's saddle creaked as he stepped down, telling the story. Hogarth saw a metallic shimmer run across the surface of Sigrod's eyes. When Otherre had finished, the old man looked at Hogarth.

"We will go inside," he said.

Hogarth had kept bachelor's quarters enough with Waco to expect a degree of untidiness, but the disruption of the Trygvesson living room harked back to the animal environment of their barbaric ancestors. The rotting buffalo hides covering the walls dripped hoary handfuls of hair over the brass-bound chest and pegged chairs beneath them. Serving as rugs were half a dozen matted bearskins with head and claws still on and covering these and the bare puncheon floor between them, from front to rear, was such a collection

167

of old bones, opened tin cans, and other rubbish as must have taken years to collect.

There was a blazing fire in the high stone fireplace, and this was the only light in the room, casting its bizarre, flickering illumination across the blank, oblivious face of Rane who sat on a grizzly pelt before the hearth, staring emptily into the flames. Sigrod saw Hogarth's eyes pass to the man.

"Surely you know Rane," he said, with clumsy mockery. "Rane, this is Hogarth, my son." Rane did not answer, and Sigrod wheeled back to Hogarth, his mouth working faintly with savage restraint. "Forgive him, Hogarth. He does not recognize anyone any more. Even his own father. Just sits there and stares and says nothing." His eyes glittered with tears, and the grin fixed on his face was ghastly.

The dogs flooded in, their hot flanks bumping against Hogarth's legs as they took their places before the fire or crouched against the wall, licking their chops, panting, growling low in their throats. Are closed the door, and the room was suddenly darker.

"Otherre told you the story," Hogarth said. "Wastewin took one steer from the Big Bit herd. I followed her. Does that sound like the rustling you're talking about?"

"One steer? Why do you want one steer?" Sigrod asked Wastewin.

She stood at the corner of a long, rough table, her lips pressed tightly together. Sigrod walked to her, the puncheon floor shaking with his great weight. Hogarth could see the anger flushing his face. He grabbed the edge of her buffalo coat, shaking her, his voice rising. "Answer me! Why one steer?"

"Sigrod," Hogarth said.

Something in his voice stopped the man. He turned, still

holding her coat. He saw the look in Hogarth's face, and for a moment a flinty humor flashed in his eyes. "What would you do if I hurt her?"

"You've got the idea," Hogarth said.

Sigrod did not answer for a moment, his breath stirring his chest and filling the room with a stertorous sound. Then he let go of Wastewin. "You are a man, Hogarth, to stay in the basin after such a beating. At least I can give you that." He scowled, walking back to the fireplace. "You are wondering why I do not show the rage you are used to. It is because I've had time to think, Hogarth. I have now realized my mistake. It is something I should have known from the beginning. Kerry Arnold merely diverted our attention with you. It's her we're fighting. It's her we've always been fighting." He made a motion with one hand. "That was her idea, going to Cheyenne for the cattle."

"We worked it out together. I was the first to suggest it."

"Don't be so blind, Hogarth! She had been thinking of it long before you came. I'm sure of that. She had only been waiting for the right man to do it. Just like the election."

"You're twisting it all around."

"Kerry is the one that's twisting it. A week ago, Hogarth, I hated you. Now, I pity you. What has happened has shown me that you are as helpless as the rest of us. Kerry has you wound around her little finger. I was deceived at first. You looked so strong, standing on your own two feet. I didn't think she could get to one like you. That's why I blamed you for what happened. But you aren't to be hated. You are to be pitied."

"You hated Kerry's father," Hogarth said. "That's why you won't accept her."

Sigrod's massive head swung till his eyes met Hogarth's squarely. They were opaque and glassy, and a little muscle twitched in his cheek. His voice changed its tone, sounding strained. "You are right about that, Hogarth. I hated her father. And she is cut from the same cloth. She can't be content with an equal share. She has to rule, just like her father. She has to sit on top of everything and own it all. She'll even own you, if she wants to. She'll suck the guts from you and leave you little and shriveled up, like George Chapel."

Hogarth did not answer him. Sigrod kept his eyes on him a moment, breathing heavily. Then he wheeled and walked to the table, sprawling on one of the crude benches, leaning his head into his hands. His age was showing suddenly. The lines in his face no longer gave it an implacable mold; the seams and crevices slackened until they were no more than loose folds about his eyes, his mouth. He looked like a tired, old man.

"So you think I'm letting my hate blind me," he muttered. "Maybe you're right. Maybe we're all blind in this basin. Maybe what has happened through all these years has twisted us till we can't see anything clearly. Do you think I like to fight, Hogarth? When I first came to this basin, there was a woman in this house. I had three fine sons and my woman, laughter and singing. It was all I wanted. One night they came and shot through the walls . . . I don't know who, just part of the whole battle here . . . and my woman was killed. The light seemed to go out then. Ever since, I seem to have been fighting. A twisted, old man, holding his sons on a leash like dogs, hated by everyone. . . ." He trailed off. He shook his head, raised it, turned to look at Wastewin. "An old man who has forgotten his manners. Give her a seat, Are. Get her something to eat, Otherre. She has had a long ride."

Are pulled back the other bench, and Wastewin walked

170

hesitantly to it. She sat down, putting her elbows on the table. All the tension drained from her, and her head drooped till they could not see her eyes. Sigrod waved his hand at a jug on the shelves. Are got it and poured liquid into a beaker of hammered silver that was green and tarnished with great age. The smell of homemade whiskey hung rawly in the air. Wastewin was reluctant to taste it.

"Go ahead," Sigrod told her. "It will revive you. Then there will be food." He leaned toward her, a strange, lost look shining in his eyes. "You are just a child, aren't you? I don't want to believe you are the rustler. It would be good to have someone in the house again that we do not hate . . . a woman in the house." He paused, as if waiting for her to speak. Then he said, "Can't you tell us who you are? Why it is only one steer?"

Wastewin had taken a drink of the whiskey, squinting her eyes till tears ran from their corners. Otherre unwrapped a haunch of venison that had already been cooked, working it onto the spit. Hogarth walked in a dragging way to a hide-seated chair, slacking into it. He wanted to let down, wanted to believe that Sigrod's changed attitude was genuine and would last. But there was something waiting about all of them. Otherre, swinging the spit over the flames, was watching Wastewin. Are, slipping out of his Mackinaw, was doing the same thing. Wastewin opened her watering eyes. The whiskey had already sent a faint flush into her face. She saw their close attention on her and shook her head.

"I cannot tell."

Sigrod hit the table. The dogs jumped up, eyes bright, tongues hanging out. He glanced at them, made a guttural sound of impatience. Hogarth saw the effort it caused him to retain his temper. He waved his hand again, and Are got him another silver beaker, pouring it full. Sigrod drained half of it, glaring at the girl.

"What can you tell us, then? What were you doing at Medicine Wheel? Some sort of singing, they said."

"The Song to the Sun," she said. "To make holy medicine for the warriors who are fighting up north. They cannot perform *Canyouny kicicipi* now. Someone must sing for them."

"*Canyouny* what?"

"*Canyouny kicicipi,*" she repeated. "The ceremony in which a young man is sent out to get war honors. It is done by Thunder Dreamer, a man with magic powers. I have seen him make rain or drive it away many times, calling upon Wakan Tanka, the Great Spirit, for his strength. In the war ceremony he goes through the camp singing battle songs. The young men gather. One of them is chosen, and he strips to breechclout and goes out to war. If he returns in triumph, the *weakicipi* is performed for him, the Victory Dance."

"*Siger!*" the old man said. "Victory. That is amazing. One would almost think you were descended from the Vikings, as we are. For though our country is Sweden, our ancestors long ago were Norsemen."

Are nodded. "There are those who say the American coast was the Helluland discovered and settled by the son of Eric the Red in ancient times."

"How else could it be?" Sigrod said. "This Wakan Tanka is the same as Odin, the supreme god. This Thunder Dreamer is like Frey, the god who presides over rain and sunshine. You even go into battle like the Vikings did. Did you ever hear of Berserker, who was so filled with battle lust he stripped off all his armor and rushed naked to the fight, defeating the enemy single-handed? And on the return from war . . . *siger* . . . the Victory Dance." He pounded his beaker on the table, turning to Hogarth. "Drink with us, Hogarth. We have found a kinswoman, a regular Valkyrie from Valhalla to fill our horns with meat and feed us with flesh of the swine."

Are filled a beaker for Hogarth. Sigrod held his up to be refilled. Hogarth could see how the whiskey was reaching the old man now. His eyes were glittering brightly, and his face was flushed. He took a long drink, clanked the beaker on the table again.

"We have our songs, too," said Sigrod thickly. "The same as your Song to the Sun, and your Thunder Dreamer chant. Rane used to be the *skuald* in this house. Now Otherre has to do it. Isn't that too bad, Hogarth? Rane can no longer sing and play as he used to. Rane can no longer do anything. Just sits there and stares. Sing us a song, *skaald,* play your *langelik* and sing us the *Bjarkmal!*"

Otherre took off his Mackinaw and got the harp-like instrument from the corner, plucking a few tentative notes on the *langelik,* bringing them into tune. Then he began singing in a strange, alien tongue. The venison was dripping juice into the fire now, hissing and spitting, and the dogs were all on their feet, watching the meat with avid eyes and slavering jowls. Sigrod was pounding his beaker in time to Otherre's shrill song. The drink and the music seemed to be releasing something wild in all the Trygvessons, something that had lain beneath the surface, despite Sigrod's effort at restraint, ever since they had entered the house. Hogarth was filled with a sense of mounting tension in the room. Wastewin must have felt the same thing. He saw a frown make a feathery etching of her forehead as she glanced with wide, dark eyes at Hogarth. Sigrod moved unsteadily down the table. Hogarth's fists clenched.

"We would like to know where those cattle have been taken and by whom," Sigrod said, his head lowering.

Wastewin's chin lifted. "I don't know."

Sigrod reached out a giant hand to clutch the front of her buckskin dress, jerking her up. "You do know! Where are they? Why is it we can never trail them past the Medicine Wheel?" He shook her. Wastewin's bare calf was yanked against the brass side of a stew pot that had been simmering on a hook within the hearth. She cried out in pain. Hogarth's whole body gathered itself involuntarily for the shift toward them. Otherre stopped plucking at the *langelik* to pull his Colt from its holster and lay it on the table before him.

"Father," said Are, "she's only a girl. . . !"

"She's only a long rider," shouted Sigrod, the restraint slipping from him swiftly in a mounting violence, and he threw her brutally back against the wall, oblivious to that bare leg once more hitting against the stew pot. "Where are they?" he roared, beating her against the wall. "Where are the cattle, and who rides with you?"

Perhaps Are's youth retained remnants of the chivalry the others had lost, for he stepped around Hogarth to jump across the room, catching his father by those immense, bunched shoulders.

"Sigrod, Sigrod, you're drunk. You can't beat a girl like you would a dog. She's a woman, Sigrod. Remember Gudrude. . . ?!"

"Are you questioning my authority!" bellowed Sigrod, releasing Wastewin to whirl about and catch Are behind the neck with one hand. The boy tried to tear free, but with a sweeping motion of his gigantic arm Sigrod spun Are across the room to crash up against the wall. There he slid down the undressed pine logs in a cloud of dust and hair shaken from the rotting buffalo robes and remained there, staring at his father in a dazed, twisted way.

Rane remained completely oblivious to this, gazing emptily into the fire. Sigrod stood glaring at Are for a moment, breathing heavily, his face the color of raw beef from the diffused blood in it. In turning back to Wastewin, his eyes crossed Hogarth in a momentary, covert way. Hogarth saw something sly in them. He realized, with a dull shock, what Sigrod's purpose was.

Otherre sat at the table, that wooden, waiting look on his face, battered fingers continuing to pluck idly at the instrument. Sigrod had turned completely back to Wastewin. She stood spread-eagled against the wall, staring intently at something on the floor. Hogarth saw it then. His six-gun lay on the grizzly pelt just behind Rane. Are had stuffed it into his belt, and it must have been torn loose when Sigrod spun him across the room. Wastewin's eyes raised to Hogarth. He allowed his head to dip faintly.

"H'g un!" cried Wastewin in a shrill, strident voice and spun away from between Sigrod and the wall. He lurched forward to catch her, but she had already snatched a long, blazing brand from the fire. It struck Rane in the face as she wheeled back with it, and he reared up with a startled, animal scream. Otherre put down the *langelik* and drove to his feet, reaching for his Colt. Hogarth was already lurching for his own weapon and knew he would be a million years too late. Then the blazing brand flew from behind Sigrod and, like a flame-tipped arrow, struck Otherre fully in the face. His roar of agony filled the room.

Hogarth was scooping up his gun and spinning toward the man. Otherre had reeled back with the pain but was now trying to recover himself, pawing blindly at his eyes with one hand and bending forward to try and line up his Colt. Hogarth's left palm made a fanning motion across the big hammer. The crash drowned all other sound for that

175

instant. Otherre grunted sickly and bent forward, still trying to bring his gun in line.

The shot caused Sigrod to release Wastewin and whirl toward Hogarth. Are was leaping from where he had been thrown against the wall. Ignoring them both, Hogarth fanned his gun again. Otherre groaned and fell forward across the table, lying on his chest there as he stubbornly tried to lift his gun.

"I can see now, Hogarth," he shouted in a agonized triumph. "I can see now."

Hogarth fanned out a third shot and saw Otherre's head jerk up to it and Otherre's Colt go off toward the ceiling. Then there was a hissing sound, and darkness fell with a shocking suddenness. Both Sigrod and Are struck Hogarth at the same time.

He went down beneath them, realizing Wastewin must have upset the kettle of stew on the fire, for that hissing rose above Sigrod's harsh shout. Hogarth rolled over in utter blackness, his gun coming against someone. The shot was muffled. The man's scream caused a shooting pain in Hogarth's eardrums, deafening him momentarily, but one of those bodies was dead weight on him now. He squirmed from beneath it, slashing blindly at the other man, rewarded by a cry of pain and a sudden release.

He gained his feet. Another body stumbled into his, and he whirled against it, bringing his gun around before he sensed, by its softness, who it was.

"Wastewin?" he gasped.

"Are?" bellowed Sigrod in an anguished way from the fireplace. "Are?"

Wastewin twisted Hogarth toward the door, and they stumbled through. His boots made a hollow clatter across the stone porch and down the steps, and it must have been heard from within. They were not half way across the compound to the horses when a vague, uncertain light flickered into being in the house, outlining the doorway. The dogs were baying crazily now and circling back and forth.

"That brand you threw must have caught on those pelts," Hogarth gasped. "The whole place is on fire."

A silhouette appeared momentarily in the illuminated rectangle of the doorway. Hogarth turned to fire, but his gun clicked on an empty chamber. Cursing, he began ejecting the empties. The man in the door stumbled across the porch, down the steps, and then weaved in a strange, mechanical run toward the timber, not even looking toward Hogarth and Wastewin.

"*Vaer dig selv nok,*" he called in a hollow monotone, staring blankly at the trees as he stumbled toward them. "*Vaer dig selv nok. . . .*"

"Rane," muttered Hogarth as the man disappeared into the trees, still calling that idiotic refrain. As they too reached the timber, another silhouette appeared in the growing light of the door, a silhouette turned grotesquely top heavy by the great weight centered in the shoulders.

"*Hogarth!*" It was Sigrod's voice, filled with the deafening thunder of those icebergs. "Hogarth! You've killed my boys. They're dead, Hogarth, and you killed them! I know you're out there. By Odin, I swear I'll hunt you till I find you, and by Frey I swear I'll make you suffer when I find you, like no tortured soul in hell has ever suffered, and then by Thor, I'll kill you, Hogarth. I'll kill you!"

Hogarth and Wastewin mounted and wheeled the horses in a run into the trees. They rode without speaking, keeping to a gallop until their horses showed signs of lagging. Then they slowed down.

He looked into her face, touched by the sun and the wind till it glowed with a wild and vivid beauty. "I think by now you know where I stand," he said.

The light left her big black eyes. They grew heavy lidded, somber. "I hope I do," she said. "After what you did today, I think I can prove to you that I'm not doing that other rustling."

"You were going east, into the badlands. Are you hiding in the Hole-in-the-Wall country?"

Her gaze fluttered. She frowned at him. "Why do you say that?"

"It's over that way. It's the most logical spot."

She shook her head. "I have never seen it."

Chapter Eighteen

They rode eastward once more, through the ageless indifference of timber-black peaks massed against the sky, through cañons without names, and across ridges whipped by a wind a million years old. And they reached the badlands again. Once into the twisted, burned land Hogarth understood why Kasna and the others had been unable to track Wastewin beyond the edge of this country.

They crossed miles of sand, whipped by a fitful wind that covered their prints in a few minutes. They pushed through endless stretches of loose crust that slithered away beneath each step, obliterating a track as soon as it was made. Wastewin's unshod pinto did not even leave the scars of an iron shoe on the rocks.

They rode the day out, with Hogarth's belly crawling from hunger and a sodden exhaustion dragging him down in the saddle, with the sun burning like fire against the back of his neck and the horses growing frantic for water that wasn't there. Then, out of a ruddy evening sky, another backbone of peaks stood straight against the heavens.

They rode in silence between the toes of the mountains, reached thin timber, a brackish stream. Wastewin followed the stream into hidden cañons, still steaming with gathered heat. Finally, the mouth of one opened into a park covered with thin grass. The timber was heavier here, and the pine scent sweetened the air.

At the far end of the park was a smoke-blackened teepee of skins. An old woman crouched before it, dressed in an open-sleeved dress of elkskin. There was a wooden bowl before her, filled with what appeared to be chokeberries. She was pounding them into a paste in a second bowl. She rose as she saw Wastewin, blinking smoke-blinded eyes.

"Kicita?" she cried shrilly.

Wastewin shook her head, rattling off something in Sioux. Then she told Hogarth: "She wanted to know if you were of the white troops."

Hogarth had pulled his horse to a stop, warily scanning the camp. "Who is she?"

"My aunt. Her name is Zinkesiwin. She is the wife of Yellow Elk."

He looked at her sharply. "Yellow Elk?"

A sardonic smile touched her lips. "Yes. Isn't that what you wanted to know? He is in the teepee, Hogarth."

"Why doesn't he come out? He's heard us."

"You will have to go in."

She led Hogarth to the teepee. He studied the rope corral under the trees. There were old droppings outside its present confines. Evidently it had once held many animals. Now, however, there were only four ratty ponies shoving restlessly against the rope — one horse, perhaps two, for carrying the camp gear. That left at most three to ride. It added up, but he still could not help the crawling sensation down the back of his neck. The old woman's eyes were fixed on him like glass beads. Wastewin pulled to a stop, slid off, handing her reins to the squaw. Hogarth dismounted, stiff from the long ride. Wastewin ducked through the opening in the teepee, holding the flap for Hogarth. It was gloomy inside, lit only by a shaft of twilight coming through the smoke hole at the top. It took his eyes a moment to accustom themselves to the gloom. Then he saw the circle of rocks, filled with gray ashes of a dead fire, and beyond that a man.

He lay on a swarthy buffalo robe with a pair of Hudson's Bay four-point blankets pulled over him. There were streaks of gray in his inky, shoulder-length hair. It was unbraided and lay like a thick, rumpled fan beneath his head. His face was yellow as jaundice, cheeks sunken, eyes glazed and feverish. One hand lay on top of the blankets, the tendons shining tranlucently through the wasted flesh.

Hogarth moved on inside and straightened up. There was a stench of grease and sweat and rotting hides. The Indian turned his head fitfully, blinking at Hogarth. Finally his glazed eyes came into focus, and he drew a rattling breath.

"Hohaha, kola," he said. He coughed, a weak, racking cough that ran through his body in a spasm and left him panting feebly.

Wastewin knelt at his side, touching him on the shoulder. Then she raised her head again, bitter irony tinging her voice. "He welcomed you to his teepee. He is so feverish he thinks you are a friend."

Hogarth moved nearer, staring down at the Indian. Sickness had wasted him away till he looked aged and shrunken. Yet Hogarth knew that he was only in his middle forties, and once must have had a powerful body.

"What happened?" he asked.

"He was wounded in a skirmish with the soldiers," she said. "He is dying. He wanted to come back to his own country. He wanted to be buried with his own people, near the Medicine Wheel. This was his hunting ground as a young man. He was born in the Big Horn Basin, on the very spot where Meeteetse now stands."

Hogarth went to one knee beside the man. "Couldn't a doctor save him?"

She shook her head. "The wound is too bad. We expected him to die before this. He would not return to the agency.

181

He would not even let me bring a doctor from Cody. It would have been useless anyway."

"What happened to the others in this camp?"

She spoke sullenly, her head down. "In the beginning there were about forty of us who escaped from the agency at Standing Rock. The soldiers followed us, and we had to fight. Yellow Elk was wounded then. The warriors, about twenty-five of them, stayed behind to keep on fighting while the girls, women, and old men ran on down here. We tried hunting at first and managed to get enough to eat. Then we ran out of powder and lead. That is why I had to go down after the steers. When we learned Lieutenant Bannister had defeated the warriors and was coming down here, the others got frightened and started back to the agency. Only Yellow Elk and Zinkasiwin and I stayed."

He studied her closely. "And you still claim you only took one steer at a time?"

She looked up at him irritably. "Any more would have left a trail too easy to follow or would have slowed me down so I would have been caught. It took the whole bunch of us several weeks to eat one steer, anyway."

"Are you sure all the others went back to the agency?"

Her lips grew thin. "You are still thinking we took those other cattle."

"Somebody is taking them. Twenty or thirty head at a time on a barefoot horse. And it's possible that that same rider has killed Charles Tremaine."

It would have taken a consummate actor to feign such genuine surprise. The coppery flesh drained from her cheeks, leaving them pale. She moistened her lips, shaking her head from side to side. When she finally spoke, her voice was low, strained.

"And you think . . . you think that was me?"

"You took a shot at Waco and me."

A violent protest leaped into her face. Her lips parted, and he expected a hot denial. But she subsided and, when she finally spoke, it was in a strained tone. "That shot I took at you was my last bullet, and I had been saving it for weeks. Why else would I go after steers this way?"

He searched her face, seeking the truth. There was something of the simple purity of the wind and the sun in this woman that made him want to believe her. She saw the doubt on his face, and the light died in her eyes.

"You don't believe me."

He shook his head, intensely confused, not knowing what to say. She spoke again, in a thin voice.

"You don't believe me, and you are going to take me back to Lieutenant Bannister."

Hogarth glanced at Yellow Elk. "Can he be moved?"

"He would die."

He raised his eyes to hers. "Then I couldn't take you from him, could I?"

Some of the color began to return to her cheeks. She moistened her lips. "You mean . . . you won't. . . ?"

He moved closer to her. "Wastewin, I used to be able to trust my feelings about people. I want to believe you now. If the barefoot rider was not you, then there is another person responsible for the disappearance of a lot of cattle, and they have to be somewhere! If I could find the western entrance to Hole-in-the-Wall. . . ."

Wastewin's eyes dropped involuntarily to Yellow Elk. Hogarth nodded. "I've been told that if anybody knew of the entrance, Yellow Elk would. Can he tell me?"

She hesitated a moment then went to her knees beside the wasted man. *"Tunka,"* she said softly. *"Tunka sila le ayahpe ya yo."*

There was more, flowing on and on. The Indian dialects had always sounded harsh and guttural to Hogarth when he had heard them before. She made music out of it. Finally, she stopped. Yellow Elk's eyes opened. They were filmed with pain and fever. Hogarth saw them make a great effort to focus. Finally, in a rattling whisper, it came.

"Pte ta tiyopa."

Hogarth waited, but there was no more. "What's that?" he asked.

"Gate of the Buffalo," Wastewin answered. "It is the entrance to Hole-in-the-Wall." She asked the Indian more, and he answered. She told Hogarth: "Yellow Elk says few know of it. Perhaps only two in the whole world. He and a friend who followed a white buffalo across those badlands when he was a youth and this was his hunting ground. The buffalo led them to this cañon, hidden in the cliffs. Beyond was a country as green as Big Horn Basin."

"This friend. Is he still alive?"

She spoke to the Indian. Yellow Elk shook his head, speaking feebly. Wastewin said: "The friend is dead. His name was Jack Dagget."

Hogarth frowned at her. "Would that be Lee Dagget's father?"

"It must be. I know Jack Dagget trapped with my father."

Hogarth settled back, running a thumb absently across his teeth, considering this. "Can he draw a map?"

There was a low-voiced conversation between Yellow Elk and Wastewin. Then she lifted the claw-like hand off the blanket and put it on the ground. The Indian was too weak to use it. She had to move it in the dirt, according to his directions. Hogarth watched the lines and circles take shape, trying to understand them. Wastewin pointed out a landmark.

184

"That is the butte shaped like mule ears, back in the badlands. From there you must head south. There will be a ridge from which you can see a dry lake bed. Beyond that, a cañon formed by the old river that once flowed into the lake. At the head of the cañon, a stone arrow made by the ancient ones who built the Medicine Wheel. Follow its direction straight against the cliff that rises to the east. You will find the Gate of the Buffalo hidden by a rock slide."

Hogarth settled back. The ride had left him exhausted. Yet he knew he had to take this chance. He felt that he was close to something, and he could not quit now.

"How long?" he asked.

"Yellow Elk says a half-day ride. But you must stay here tonight. You have gone too long already without rest."

Hogarth knew she was right. He ached all over with exhaustion, and he was weak with hunger. He nodded in agreement, and Wastewin went out for a moment. He could hear her talking with the older woman, and then she ducked back in.

"We will fix something to eat. All we have is pemmican and some soup, but it will help."

She shed her buffalo coat. Her buckskin jacket and leggins were soiled, but they had been pure white at one time, and they clung faithfully to the shape of her lithe body. She was not as full as Kerry through the bust and hips, but she was still sweetly curved. Her figure held a girlish appeal that Kerry's could never have, something fresh and new and untouched.

Bone weary, Hogarth lay back in the heap of buffalo robes and tattered blankets, watching her through half-closed eyes. He realized he was taking a distinct pleasure in each quick motion of her supple body, as she knelt to build a fire in the circle of rocks. It was not the same thing he felt when watching Kerry's body, not the sudden fire of desire, the burning need to possess. And yet there was no lack of physical attraction. He saw her breasts, high and firm and round, outlined by the buckskin jacket, and knew that here was a woman who could arouse a man in her own way. Then how was it a different way? What gave it such affinity with the cleansing touch of the wind and the pristine scent of the pines? Was it her youth, the hint of untouched purity that a mature woman could never have, no matter what else she offered?

Hogarth suddenly realized how much he had taken for granted. Maybe that was it. Maybe he had put too much faith in her innocence when it wasn't really there. He remembered the savagery of her when he had first caught her at Medicine Wheel and the sudden withdrawal with which she met the Trygvessons. There was more than youth and sweetness to her. A rush of apprehension coursed through him. He rose quickly and moved to the door. The old woman was not in sight. The night had come, filling the park with a sooty darkness. The wind whined like a cur in the trees, and the chill air was freighted with a new tang. He stooped through the flap and went to Wastewin.

"Where is your aunt?" he asked.

"She went down for water."

He glanced at her, barely visible beside him, standing so close he could feel that warmth of her body against him, scented with the same perfume as the forest, wild and piney and strangely exciting. He felt like a fool. Yet he could not down his suspicions. He had wanted to find out about this place too eagerly. He hadn't asked enough questions, hadn't taken enough precautions.

"Maybe she's gone out to get those others," he said.

"Maybe."

Her voice sounded husky. He realized she was taking a sly relish from his disturbance. It was the child in her, and he wheeled toward her, grabbing her arm.

"This is no time to play," he said. "Tell me the truth. If she's gone after some others, you and I will go back to Lieutenant Bannister right now. If you're joking with me, I think I'll take you over my knee and whale you."

It was the first time he had ever heard her laugh. It was like the gurgle of a stream. "I guess you'll have to whale me. Here is my aunt."

He glanced sharply at the rustle of pine needles beneath shuffling moccasins. The old woman appeared, frowning at them, then ducked into the teepee with a bullhide pail of water. He waited a long time, listening, waiting. Nothing happened. Finally, feeling more foolish than ever, he said: "I guess I deserve it. It's what I get for not trusting you, after you trusted me."

She did not move for a moment. She spoke in a low voice. "You are a strange man, Hogarth. I would hate to be the man to fight you. Yet, when you are with a woman. . . ."

She trailed off, and he let go of her arm. "What about a woman?"

She didn't answer. She looked at him a moment longer then turned quickly and ducked through the opening. He took one more glance around the meadow and followed her. They ate soup and pemmican, and it filled his belly, anyway. And it made him drowsy, which was dangerous. He kept listening for horses in the night, for some alien sound on the wind. Suddenly, he was aware of Wastewin's steady gaze, studying him.

"I cannot help thinking of Sigrod," she said at last.

"Do you feel that we ran away?"

She shook her head. "I know how it was, Hogarth. You

187

wanted to get me away from there. But I know, too, that you couldn't just stay there for the purpose of killing again."

He lowered his eyes, staring at the ground. "The whole thing was twisted, somehow, from the start. I had no basic cause for a quarrel with them. Under any other circumstances we might. . . ," — he broke off, making a gesture with his hand, as if seeking the words — "what I mean is, their strength, their courage, their individuality. . . ."

"You could have admired," she finished for him. "You are beginning to see, then."

His face raised. "See what?"

"What it is you sought here, Hogarth? I know more of what was going on down there in the basin than you think. I could see the way you came in with nothing but a few cattle and your wits and your strength and began to take control. You have gained control now, haven't you? One more step and you'll be in the big saddle. And then what will you have?"

It came from him automatically. "Something I've worked for all my life."

"What?" she said. "A big rich house you won't spend much time in? A grasping, ruthless woman who won't be satisfied till she owns the whole county, the whole state? A crew so big you won't even know them personally? A complete lack of friends because they'll no longer trust you? Surrounded by fawning, fork-tongued weaklings, because you've had to kill off all the strong, square ones like the Trygvessons who refused to knuckle under?"

"Wastewin. . . !"

"And when you do reach that position, what will you have?" She swept one arm out to point through the trees. "Look down there. I own as much land as you do. I can ride on it or drink its water or gather siptois from the arrow-leaf.

The sunshine is mine, the sky, the trees, the earth."

"You speak as an Indian," he said. "A white man needs more."

"Why?" she asked. "Have you ever had any more, before this, in all your life?"

A rueful smile touched his lips, and he shook his head slowly, staring at her in wonderment. "No."

"Are you as happy now as when you rode with your friend and the whole world was your pasture?"

Memories surged through him in a swiftly growing tide. Finally, he shook his head again and abruptly turned the conversation around.

"What will you do when Yellow Elk is gone?" he asked.

"Zinkasiwin and I will go back to the agency. We could not survive out here for long. This uprising will not give the Indians freedom, anyway. Soon they will all be back on the reservation. I think they realize that, in their hearts. It is but the last despairing effort of a defeated people to win back their old lands, their old life. But they lost that life years ago, at the battle of the Little Big Horn. They may have massacred Custer, but it was the beginning of the end. Sitting Bull has told me that many times. We are a conquered people."

Her eyes were blank and fatalistic, her face tilted down till the shadows made deep hollows beneath her cheekbones. It made her look infinitely Indian, completely primitive. It took him back to the first time he had heard her singing.

"We have lost our freedom," she said softly, finally.

He had no answer for that. The fire burned low, and he must have dozed off. He didn't know how long he slept. He came awake with a start to find the fire had died, and the teepee was dark. He could hear the steady breathing

189

of the others, somewhere in the blackness. He rose and went outside. Stars spangled the sky, and the intense chill made him shiver. He stalked about the meadow, with the horses snorting and whinnying in the corral. Finally he returned to the teepee and rolled into a buffalo robe and slept again. He woke the second time to the acrid scent of wood smoke and the pale light of dawn. They had pemmican and soup once more, and then he donned his Mackinaw. He stood above Yellow Elk, wishing he could do something for the man. But it was as Wastewin had said. The man was obviously too far gone to move, and much beyond the limited help Hogarth could give him.

The old woman packed some more of the tasteless pemmican into a greasy buckskin for him. Wastewin went out to help him saddle up. There was a dewy sweetness to the morning, and the birds filled the air with music. He wondered how it might be to live like this, free as those birds, unfettered by the conventions and the drives of the life he had known, untainted by all the obscure clashes and suspicions of the basin he had come from. He slid his latigo through the cinch ring, tugged it tight, aware of Wastewin watching him closely. When he turned to her, she put her hand impulsively to his arm and said: "I should go with you today."

"Yellow Elk needs you," he said.

Her hand grew heavier on his arm. She was looking up into his face, a strange expression in her eyes. "I hate to think of you in those badlands alone."

"Do you?"

For a moment neither of them spoke. The wind boomed defiantly through the pines and then died. Then she spoke again in a low voice.

"That woman. You are in love with her?"

He smiled at her. "What makes you ask that?"

"I did not ask. I could see. You are in love with her. And you don't know."

"Don't know what?"

"The Indians know. Up at the agency. They say she is evil, a woman too like a man."

She pronounced it with all the sober naïveté of a little girl. It took him completely off guard. He stared at her face, the smoky eyes, the full underlip. And then he understood. He smiled again, wryly.

"I think you're jealous."

She stiffened. A scarlet flush ran into her face. Her pupils dilated, big and black, so like a cat's in rage that for a moment he almost thought she would spit at him. Then, without a word, she wheeled and walked swiftly back to the teepee. He couldn't help grinning to himself, watching her go across the meadow. Her hips were swinging in her angry stride. Below the fringe of her jacket they were ripe and round, and they did a little dance against the grease-slick buckskin of her tight leggins. Maybe she was still a little girl in some ways, but the rest of her was all woman.

Chapter Nineteen

It was the vast barrenness again, with the yellow dust blowing forever against him. He had to stop every fifteen minutes and clean the clogged nostrils of his bay. He kept seeing mirages dancing on the horizon, cattle herds and beckoning lakes.

Near noon he found the mule-ear butte and turned south from there. He was surprised at how the pemmican had revived his energy and munched at some more of the tasteless food. He saw a ridge ahead and topped it. Before him he could recognize the pale oval of the ancient lake. Circling it, he came upon the cañon the river had cut out of this sandstone a thousand years ago, or perhaps a million, and rode on south through its crimson-striped walls. It opened into a land turned to a wild labyrinth by erosion. Deep gullies and tortured cañons ran in every direction, an endless maze in which a man could lose himself in five minutes. And no stone arrow.

He got down to rest his horse and stood in the meager shade of the cañon wall. Doubts had been probing him ever since he had left, and now they burgeoned into full bloom. Just what kind of gullible fool was he? He had taken her word. He had taken the sweet softness of her face for simple sincerity, had let her send him out here on a wild-goose chase, giving her all the time in the world to pack up and get Yellow Elk out of there to a new hiding place, from where it would start all over again, the unshod horse, the rustling, the killing. He had let her weave a spell of pine-scented wildness and primitive beauty and childish naïveté, and he had fallen under it and played the fool.

Then he shook his head. It had been more than her spell. All the things he had put together didn't add up to her. Every time he had seen her, she had taken only one steer. And there had been no sign of large bunches of cattle around the camp.

He had to finish this up, one way or another. He stifled his impulse to turn back and mounted again. He spent a precious hour finding a trail to the top of the cañon walls. From this height he could see the surrounding country, serrated by the maze of cañons and gorges. And in one, pointing due east, was a line of limestone slabs as big as those forming the Medicine Wheel. Slabs laid in the shape of a giant arrow.

He descended to the cañon bottom, traced out the gorge in which the arrow lay, and rode to it. From here he traveled due east, up out of the gorge again, till he reached the plateau. Now he could see mountains again, blue-black against the steel-colored sky. The late sun was turning the rocks crimson when he left the maze of gorges and ran up against a great sandstone escarpment that ran north and south as far as he could see.

A half mile to the south he saw where the escarpment had caved in, forming a rock slide. He approached till he was a few feet from the fringe of tumbled rocks and yellow shale. There was no sign of a cañon. It merely looked as if the face of the cliff had been shaken loose. He hunted till he found a way to the top. Then, dismounting, he began to lead his horse up the rocks and shale. Half way up he started a small avalanche and almost went down with it. The echoes rumbled against the cliff and more of the face slid down from above, barely missing him. He hugged the side, fighting a panic-stricken horse, till it ceased. Then he continued to pick his way on up.

The top of the vast slide must have been two hundred feet high. Only when he reached it did he realize why he hadn't sighted the cañon mouth from below. The entrance of the cañon was literally a hole in the face of the cliff with a stone bridge on top a hundred feet thick. The cone-shaped rock slide ran almost up to the bridge, completely hiding the tunnel from anyone standing below. He made his way laboriously down the back of the slide, starting a dozen more miniature avalanches before he reached the cañon. He passed under the stone bridge and saw the sky above once more. Then he followed the cañon for a mile.

Ahead of him, in the last of the sunlight, Hogarth saw the valley. It was as Yellow Elk had said — as green as Big Horn Basin, stretching for miles into the sun-purpled mountains that ringed its eastern side. On the slopes, cropping at the stirrup-high grass, were the cattle. He rode slowly into the first bunch. They were branded with Charles Tremaine's Big Bit. Beyond, bedding down in a coulee, was another small bunch with George Chapel's Tee Broom on their sleek flanks.

Hogarth could see more in the distance, but he did not bother riding any farther. He had found what he'd been searching for. He knew it would be useless for him to try rounding them up alone and driving them back. It would probably take all the men in the basin to collect and drive back the number of cattle that had been brought out here through the past years. Night had come, and he knew it would be pushing both himself and the horse too hard to attempt a return trip. He found a camp site in the timber and unlashed his blanket roll. He picketed his horse, threw the saddle down for a pillow, and rolled in. He was dead tired and fell asleep almost immediately.

It was no longer dark when he awoke. The sky was growing pearly with dawn, and somewhere a chat was scolding. But it wasn't the bird that had awakened him. The earth seemed to be trembling. He rolled over, staring toward the cliffs. A distinct bawling came from that direction. It was a familiar sound — not the sound of drifting cattle but of a herd being driven.

He rolled out and saddled his grazing horse quickly. There was not even time to roll up his blankets. The smell of dust was in the air, and the bawling was louder. He swung into the saddle and pulled his animal into the cover of scrub timber.

The first steer rounded the turn in the coulee below, running. More followed, kicking up dust like yellow smoke. There were about thirty head, with Hogarth's own Rocker T on their sweaty flanks.

The sight filled him with a tight breathlessness, a savage sense of triumph. He had come to the end of his trail. He moved down through the timber, pulling his Ward-Burton from the saddle boot as the rider appeared. It was Lee Dagget.

Hogarth felt his hands tighten around the rifle in surprise. Then he thumped heels to his bay, driving it out of the timber and off the bank of the coulee into its sandy bottom. Dagget saw Hogarth just as he reached the sand. The man pulled his horse up so sharply it squealed and sat back on its haunches. In the next instant his hand jerked out, snapping the reins against the side of the animal's neck, and the horse started to wheel around. It was merely reflex action, however, for he had already seen the rifle in Hogarth's hands, pointing at him. He stopped the horse's wheeling motion and held it on a tight rein, fiddling and fretting in the sand. His weight sank back into the saddle, and he sat glaring balefully at Hogarth. Dust lay in a chalky film on the man's Levi's and bearskin coat; his face was caked with it, except where sweat had washed it away, running down the seams about his mouth and at the corners of his eyes.

Hogarth let the last of the cattle run by, bawling and snorting. Then, carefully, he reined his horse toward Dagget. The man did not speak as he approached. Neither did Hogarth. The surprise was drained out of him now, and he was piecing it together, seeing the logic of it, wondering why it had not been apparent to him before.

From the first it obviously had not been ordinary rustling. When he had found the cattle here last night, it should have become clear to him. Only a man with strange motives would bring cattle here, leave them, not even try to sell them. A motive like hate, or bitterness, or revenge. A motive as warped and intense as Hogarth had seen in Dagget's mind that night in Kerry's kitchen.

He stopped his horse five feet from the man. "And I thought you loved Kerry," he said.

He saw the whipped look pinch the man's face, more subdued this time. Dagget let it die before he spoke thinly, sarcastically: "What's that got to do with it?"

"Maybe you loved her once," Hogarth said. "But this is the other side of the coin. You wanted her so much it warped you when you couldn't have her. It twisted you."

The man's eyes were smoldering. "You're crazy."

"I think you're the crazy one," Hogarth said. "Why else would you take this kind of revenge? Trying to ruin everything she's worked for in that basin. Keeping the ranchers at each other's throats with this rustling. Draining them of beef so they could never get their heads above water."

Some of the anger left Dagget. That malicious smile came to his lips. "You really got it all figured out, ain't you?"

"What did you hope to gain?" Hogarth asked. "Was it just revenge, or did you think you'd keep anybody else from having her this way? Maybe you even hoped she'd turn back to you when you'd pulled her down to your level."

"Did I?" There was mockery in the man's voice.

Hogarth felt a corrosive anger growing in him. "It's made you ugly inside, Dagget. I should have seen it that night in Kerry's kitchen. I should have realized what it would make you do."

"Should you?"

The two men were so engrossed in each other that they were completely unaware of the quiet approach of the rider until Sigrod's booming roar shattered the peace of the morning meadow. "By Odin, I found not one but two rustlers! I always suspected you were mixed up in this, Hogarth."

Startled, Hogarth reacted immediately, wheeling his horse with a jerking motion that made his Ward-Burton swing in a violent arc that knocked Dagget backwards, his feet leaving the stirrups. He rolled off the pony backwards and fell to the ground. Stumbling to his feet, Dagget took a staggering step forward, trying to reach for his gun, and then fell on his face, senseless.

Hogarth was already whirling to his left. Sigrod drove his great white stallion in a wild run at Hogarth, firing into the dust before Hogarth's rearing mount. The gunshots startled the cattle into a running, bawling mill, raising a pall of dust that obscured Hogarth, but the rider charging from the trees was plain enough.

"*Siger,* Hogarth!" he bellowed. "*Siger!*" His gun flamed as he rode down on him with a twisted, raging face.

Hogarth fired at the stallion, saw it jerk and stagger with the slug, and raised his rifle a little higher. Firing again, he saw Sigrod reel sideways in the saddle. Then he had to rein his own horse aside from the thundering, stumbling white beast. Sigrod's gun loomed in his vision, and he ducked aside, realizing the man had thrown it. He tried to shift his horse away as Sigrod came hurtling at him. But the man's gigantic body struck Hogarth, wild Viking screams deafening him as they went to the ground.

Sigrod's great weight crushed Hogarth's breath from him. Gasping with the pain of it, rifle torn from his hand by the violent fall, he fought to roll from beneath the grizzled giant. He gained his feet, but Sigrod followed him up, bleeding from the chest where Hogarth's bullet had caught him, roaring his vengeance to Odin and Snorre. Hogarth knew the mistake of trying to stand up to the man and allowed the savagery of Sigrod's attack to drive him backward, grunting spasmodically as one of the man's great fists almost knocked him from his feet.

He had not reckoned with the limestone slabs, however, and found himself halted suddenly, with the feel of rough stone at his back. Before he could wheel away, Sigrod had pinned him there and was mauling him. Hogarth put his head down, driving his blows with all his vicious strength into Sigrod's midsection. He could feel the lithic contraction of stomach muscles in the man's belly, inches thick, so hard they hurt his hands with each blow, and realized with a sickening sense of futility how little effect it was having on Sigrod. The Norseman merely expelled a little air at each blow and continued to bellow like a maddened bull, bleeding all over Hogarth as he drove him back against the limestone.

Blinded, gasping beneath the deadly ferocity of the attack,

Hogarth reeled to one side from a blow. Sigrod's knee came into his groin, and he fell backward into darkness. Spun around that way, trying to keep his feet, with the other man following him on back, Hogarth went into the limestone cliff again. Then his face was driven harder against the stone as Sigrod crashed in behind him. He screamed with the agony of a crushed nose and flesh ground against battered cheekbone. The sound held a hollow, muted tone. He tried to twist away once more, kicking, butting, striking in a blind orgasm of agonized reaction. He managed to whirl from between Sigrod and the wall of the cliff only to come up against another jutting outcropping. This wall of limestone shuddered faintly to his violent fall against it, and he heard the dim crunch of rock against rock. Sigrod's crushing, suffocating, roaring weight was thrown into him again. A blow knocked his head back. His bleeding face turned upward for that instant, and he saw what that crunching sound had been.

There was a slab of limestone at the edge of the cliff wall. It had slipped and was held precariously by only a crumbling tip. At each spasmodic jar of Hogarth's body against the side wall, that slab of limestone quivered perceptibly. Hogarth still tried to block Sigrod's savage attack, and his swift, vicious expedience was useless in that confined space. One of Sigrod's blows knocked his head back against the stone cliff again. Groaning sickly, he saw the slab quiver above him once more. It was just a matter of time. Then he realized it was his only chance. He could not last much longer and, when his resistance ceased, Sigrod would kill him. This was the only way open to him now.

He lashed a blow into Sigrod's face. The giant grunted, knocked back far enough so that Hogarth could push himself away from the wall. Then Sigrod recovered and carried him back up against it with a terrible, driving lunge at his stomach. Retching with it, Hogarth heard the crunch of stone on stone again. He bent over, shouting in hoarse agony with the pain of the blows about his head which he had to take in that position, and butted Sigrod away once more. The man came back with one knee rising that caught Hogarth in the face, straightening him and knocking him back against the wall. Through the giddy vortex of blind agony, he heard the scrunching sound again. He put his hands flat against the wall, managed to get a bent leg between himself and Sigrod, kicking out. It pushed the giant outwards, spasmodically. Hogarth was too weak to follow. He sagged against the limestone wall, waiting for Sigrod to come back in, hoping it would be this time, knowing he could not last much longer.

"Siger!" roared the Viking, and his body crashing against Hogarth did it. Hogarth felt the wall of the cliff shake with the force. With his head turned upward, he heard the crunching stone, saw the slab quiver, start to slide off. With what was almost a gasp of thanks, he allowed his feet to slide from beneath him, catching Sigrod's arm. The man went down over him willingly, still slugging at his head. Then Sigrod's bestial screams turned to a shout of agony as the stone slab hit him. His body was borne on top of Hogarth in a rush of resilient, crushing irresistible weight. It was like sinking into a bog for Hogarth. He had a sense of that infinite weight atop him, pushing him down. There was a palpable, physical suction to unconsciousness, pulling at him like viscid, gluey mud.

Hogarth fought back the darkness, struggling, keeping his eyes open, pulling himself back from that black bog with the same sucking sensation. Sigrod was lying across him, the limestone slab pinning them both to the earth. It had struck the Norseman's head, crushing it in, and blood matted his pale mane of grizzled hair. Hogarth started squirming, working himself from beneath Sigrod, until finally, with a gasp, he had pulled himself free. He leaned weakly against the cliff wall, gingerly touching the purpling bruises of his face, dabbing futilely at sticky, caking blood.

There were still a few cattle left in the clearing, tranquilly browsing at the sparse buffalo grass. Dagget's barefoot paint stood a few feet from the man's sprawled body. Dagget was slowly coming to, shaking his head, and looking around with blurry eyes. Then, as he began to focus, he saw Hogarth and near him Sigrod's body.

"Kerry'll thank you for that," he rasped. "That man killed her father."

"How can you be sure?" Hogarth asked him in a shaky voice.

"Who else could it have been?" Dagget asked, and his battered face grimaced into a sly leer.

"I'm taking you back to Meeteetse on that barefoot pony."

There was no anger on Dagget's face. Only that sly, malicious leer.

"Got a quirly?" he asked.

"Not for you."

"Better give me one. I'm a chain smoker. I get nervous without 'em. Be dangerous to have a nervous prisoner."

"I'll be nervous, too," Hogarth said, pushing himself away from the cliff. "And I have the gun."

Chapter Twenty

They faced a long ride back. At the rock slide Dagget was ahead of Hogarth and automatically took a different trail out than Hogarth had followed in. It was much easier and well worn and got them over the slide without starting any avalanches. They were in the badlands again, with the yellow dust whipping their faces raw and the sun drawing the sweat from them till their clothes clung like paste to their backs. Again Dagget followed a trail different from the one Hogarth had used. They did not pass the stone arrow or the lake but traveled due west, across a trackless waste of sand and then into a maze of gullies and gorges where the shale and talus slithered from beneath the animals' hoofs like something alive.

Before noon Hogarth began to grow dizzy and a stabbing pain through his temples was blinding him every few minutes. He knew it was the heat and the grueling exhaustion and tried to hide it from Dagget. But the man was sending his sly little glances, and Hogarth knew he was only waiting for a break.

By noon the horses were spooky and frantic with the need for water, and it was a constant battle to keep them from growing unmanageable. Then the Big Horns swam out of the steely haze, dark blue on the horizon, beckoning. They soon reached them and rose gratefully into the shade of the timber. A mile farther on they found a stream chuckling down from the peaks. Hogarth had to fight to keep from throwing himself into the water as Dagget did. He drank carefully, his rifle beside him, his attention focused on Dagget.

The peaks rose ahead of them, gigantic, forbidding, tier upon tier. The artillery of the wind boomed constantly through distant pines. For a while it was up-and-down riding, forcing the jaded horses against the steep slopes or fighting the downhill drag and the tricky shale. Then Dagget led through a saddle and into a pass that became a cañon, dank with the smells of cold earth and stone. All this time Dagget had been watching.

Hogarth's horse was stumbling and wheezing. He knew he had pushed it hard these last days; it had done a lot more traveling than Dagget's animal and was beginning to break under the strain. Dagget had not missed that, either.

In the late afternoon they passed Medicine Wheel. They rode far below the ridge, the buffalo skull winking like a pinpoint of chalk from the shadows of the valley. After that they began to descend. Each ridge was lower than the last, each pass dropping down. And then just one of those things occurred.

Hogarth had been concentrating on Dagget, watching his every move. He was completely unprepared for the picket-pin squirrel darting across the trail from a nest of choke-berry. Hogarth's bay, nervous with exhaustion, squealed and reared high. It almost pitched Hogarth. He lunged against the saddle horn to stay aboard, sawed at the bit to bring the horse back down. He had to swing the rifle away from Dagget.

Even as the forehoofs struck ground again, Hogarth saw the man savagely reining his animal around. Hogarth tried to recover, tried to jerk the rifle into line and snap the bolt. But Dagget's horse was already spinning into the bay. They struck with a wheezing, meaty sound. The bay staggered backward, knocked off balance, and then spilled. Hogarth tried to kick free as it fell. He lost the rifle in the fall, but he couldn't help it. He hit hard, rolling away to keep from being pinned beneath the horse. He came to a stop, sprawled out on his belly, and saw the rifle ten feet from him. Dagget was wheeling his horse toward the gun, already bent forward to jump off after it.

Hogarth scrambled to one knee, pawing for his six-shooter. When Dagget saw that Hogarth would have that out before he had reached the rifle, he spun his horse again and spurred it headlong into the timber. Hogarth had his gun out, firing. But Dagget was already cut off by the trees, a fluttering shape through the tall trunks.

Hogarth jumped to his feet, still shaken by the fall, looking around for his bay. It had scrambled to its feet and was running downslope. He knew it was too tired to run far and started downhill after it. He was exhausted and almost pitched full length a dozen times. But at last he reached the bottom and saw the bay ahead. It had slowed to a nervous walk, shying and breaking into a trot every few feet, then slowing down again. Hogarth realized he still had his gun in his hand and put it away. He moved after the horse at a walk, not wanting to frighten it away by running up behind. He finally caught up with the spooky beast and got hold of the reins. It almost pitched him when he swung aboard, but he booted it into a run before it could really buck. It had no bottom left and soon began stumbling and slowed to a trot again. He had to fight it to force it upslope.

He managed to reach the last ridge between him and the basin. From here he could see Dagget again, a tiny figure in the patchwork sweep of the basin below. The man was not using the Meeteetse Trail but was heading due west. The only thing in that direction was Kerry's Big Dipper.

It sent a stab of fear through Hogarth. He knew he could not hope to catch the man on this horse. There was only one chance left him. With dusk closing in, Simms might be coming out to nighthawk the herd.

He turned the horse laterally downslope, heading in a northerly direction. In ten minutes, he reached the Rocker T fence. It was near the southeast corner of his spread, and he knew there was a poor man's gate a quarter of a mile to the west. But he couldn't waste that precious time. He hitched the bay to the fence then crawled through the barbed wire. Five minutes of stumbling through the lush-grassed lowlands of his spread brought him to the top of a rise. Ahead, gathered in a coulee, was a big cut of his steers. A rider was heading for the timber beyond. Hogarth shouted and waved, and the rider turned and spurred his horse back. It was Simms, coming up at a run, jumping off his animal, his leathery face breaking into a million wrinkles with his jubilant grin. He clapped Hogarth on both shoulders, shouting wildly. Then he saw Hogarth's mauled visage.

"My God, you'd better get to the doc. Whatever happened to you? Your wife's been out looking everywhere for you."

"I have no time. Dagget's the one on the barefoot pony, Simms. I'm right behind him now. I need a fresh horse. He's headed for the Big Dipper."

"Kerry!"

Hogarth was already swinging up on the squat man's dun. "He's in love with her, Simms. He wanted her, and she wouldn't have him. He was taking out some kind of crazy revenge. And now he's headed there."

"Are you sure. . . ?"

"He's twisted, Simms. I'm afraid of what he's up to now. I've got to get there. My bay is at the fence, southeast corner. Maybe it'll get you to the shack."

Even as he shouted this, he was wheeling the dun and kicking it into a headlong run across the meadows. He reached the poor man's gate and tore the wires free without dismounting. Then he booted the dun into a dead run toward the Big Dipper.

As he rode, his fear for Kerry grew. He remembered the doubts he had known when he had last seen her, the anger with which he had left, and a bitter self-recrimination flooded him. If anything happened to her now, he would feel to blame as much as anyone. She had kept her faith in him, had stood beside him when he needed her most. And he felt somehow that he had failed her. Why had he let the lies of others fill him with those ugly suspicions? The twisted motives driving each one of them were so obvious. The Trygvessons with their blind hate going back through the years had been blaming her for things for which she was not even responsible. Dagget, with his warped love, had wanted to destroy her if he couldn't have her. Even Wastewin, telling Hogarth that Kerry was evil, came from a girlish jealousy, venting itself in childish lies.

He had let it taint him and had very nearly let it drive him from her. Now the fear of what lay in Dagget's twisted mind stabbed at him like a knife. He spurred the horse till the rowels were red with blood, crossing timbered hills, jumping the horse over a snake fence that marked the Big Dipper's boundary, and racing through the bottomlands where Big Dipper cattle were grazing and bedding down. He finally reached the flat where the house lay.

It was full night now, and he could see light spilling through the bottle windows of the bunkhouse, illuminating Joe Hide's cutting horse where it stood by the hitch rail. Beyond was the big house, rock-studded, hip-roofed, with the yellow squares of the windows gleaming against the night. And no horse in front.

Hogarth ran the dun to the dusty tie rings by the porch and dropped off without hitching it. He ran up the steps and thrust open the door without knocking. He stopped there, eyes swinging down the room until he saw Kerry. She was sitting straight up in one of the leather chairs by the fireplace, a book in her lap, saffron brows arched in surprise.

She was wearing the green dress again, so dark against her white skin. The light burned like a subdued fire against her Titian hair. She saw his rumpled, dust-caked clothes, his haggard, beaten face, and the surprise was swept away by sharp concern. She put the book aside, rose, and rushed to him. "Bob, what happened to your face?"

"Kerry, is Dagget here?"

A shadow crossed her face. "In the bunkhouse, I suppose."

"No, I mean *here*." He glanced around then shook his head. "I must have beat him. His horse was tired. I got a fresh one. We've only got a couple of minutes."

"Bob, what are you talking about?"

"It's him on the barefoot pony, Kerry. I found the cattle. I know everything."

His hands were on her arms as he spoke, holding tight. He saw an unidentifiable expression come into her face. Her eyes went blank, and all the softness left her cheeks. They had a sharp, chiseled look. She seemed to be searching for something in his face, her eyes narrow, opaque.

"You don't look shocked!" she said at last.

His shoulders now recoiled a little. "I guess I'm not, really. I hadn't suspected it would turn out this way, I'll admit. But now that I understand it all, it seems logical."

The glow began to return to her eyes. "Then you *do* understand?"

"I guess I do. If a man wants a woman bad enough, he'll do anything."

"Bob," she breathed, "I thought it might be that way. But I wasn't sure. I saw how badly you wanted to get out on your own. Something that had been pent up inside of you for a lifetime. I saw what you were willing to do to get there, and I thought it was something in you that would allow you to understand. It was the same way with me, Bob. How could it be different? I told you how it was, how we lived. You can't give all that up easily. When you've been on top, nothing else will ever satisfy you again."

He looked wanly at her, his mind trying to adjust itself to the words. Her cheeks were beginning to flush, and that silvery glitter was in her eyes. He had seen that same look on her face before, in triumph.

"Kerry, what are you saying?"

"I'm saying we can have it together, Bob. More land than you can ride, more cattle than you can count, this house filled with people again. Big people. Senators, congressmen, presidents, kings. Did I tell you we had a king here once? It will be like that again. There's a fortune in those cattle at Hole-in-the-Wall. Just a few at a time, thirty here, twenty-five there . . . but it's added up."

He began to feel sick. He didn't want to understand all the implications of what she was saying. He could feel his mind trying to block out her words, but it was becoming too plain. There was an evil look on her face. She was speaking swiftly, excitedly.

"Of course, it wasn't all for the money we could get from the beef. The main thing was to keep the other members of the cooperative pitted against each other. They would have become too strong if something hadn't been done to keep them down, to keep them fighting among themselves.

This has bled them till they don't have the strength to stand alone, yet they're too suspicious of each other to stand together. At the same time it's built up my strength. With those cattle at Hole-in-the-Wall, and the land I can salvage from the others, I'll be the only one left in the basin."

As she went on talking, he stared emptily into her face, knowing the same wonder he had known with Dagget. He asked himself why he had not seen this warped drive in her before. He could remember that glitter in her eyes, that flush in her cheeks when she had first talked to him of her former life in the basin. Why hadn't he seen all the little signs along the way? Could desire blind a man that much?

"It's ready to fall apart," she was saying. "One push will topple the whole thing. The Trygvessons are beaten now. Chapel's mortgaged to the hilt. He'll go under this winter. Karnes is already on our side with enough beef to meet the old contracts. The only thing that kept me from moving before you came was the Trygvessons. But that's been taken care of now. You've proved that you can stand against them, Hogarth."

"And Tremaine?" His voice had a dull metallic sound.

Her eyes widened in surprise, then her underlip took on a pouting shape. "That was an accident. Dagget told me that Tremaine and Kasna might have seen him."

"When I was waiting in the Bullhorn that day, Tremaine started to tell me something he had found out on this rustling. Was that why he had to be killed?"

"Dagget went to see him that night. There was no other way. He had come too close to the truth."

Hogarth drew a thin breath. "Why Waco?"

"He was too near to you," she said. "Dagget felt he would ruin all of our plans and he was becoming a wedge between you and I." Her indrawn breath held the same weary resignation as her voice. She waved a hand at the room. "I suppose it would be out of the question to ask that you accept . . . this?"

"After Waco?" he said acridly.

She shrugged. "I suppose not."

It was an effort for Hogarth to draw in a breath. He dragged the words up from the depths of him, as if he were pulling on a heavy weight. "Waco was right. I wanted to be my own boss so much it blinded me. I wanted to get out on my own so bad I was willing to do business with a lot of slimy people I wouldn't have spoken to on the street before. I thought I was buying independence, and I was really selling out everything I ever believed in."

She stepped away from him, her mouth open.

"You made a mistake, Kerry. When I said I knew everything, I didn't mean I knew about you. I thought it was *all* Dagget."

Her eyes were wide open. Her face was pale. She moistened her lips, taken completely off guard. He saw the distinct effort to recover ripple through her face. When she spoke, her voice was strained.

"Then . . . you *are* shocked?"

"I don't think that's quite the word," he said, laughing in spite of himself. "I just feel dead inside."

She stepped to him again, grasping his arms. "Bob, don't be like that. You're grown up now. Maybe it shatters a few illusions, but you can take that. We've done it together this far. We can't stop now. You've got to know how wonderful the rest of it can be."

"And lie some more, and cheat, and kill?"

"Bob, don't be a fool. You're the only man I ever wanted. I admit I was playing them all for what I could get. Chapel and Karnes, and even Dagget. But I had to. It's the only

210

way a woman can fight. But not you, Bob. It was real with you."

"Nothing's real with you, Kerry."

"It is, it's. . . !"

Something desperate had entered her voice. She was using her body, the way she had before, arching it toward him so that her breasts stood out, round and bold, so that the curves of her thighs strained at the green skirt. He could feel the heat lick through him like a flame as she pulled herself against him. Her hands were digging into his arms, and her silken curves burned against him from knees to chest.

Her head was thrown back, her eyes half closed, her lips parted in that old look of passion. Desire crept through him, overwhelming him so he couldn't stop her when she lifted herself for his kiss. Her lips fused with his, and the lust was like a roaring in his head.

Then a wave of pure disgust swept over him. Because that was all it had ever been, a lust so deep that he had mistaken it for love. And she had done it too often before, had used that lust, had used her body to get what she wanted from him, holding out its promise, tantalizing him, leading him on, giving a little, but never all, giving just enough to keep him coming back for more.

He took his lips free, twisted her hands from his arms, and stepped back. She was panting heavily. A little pulse beat raggedly in the hollow of her neck.

"No, Kerry," he said.

The brilliant glitter went out of her face. She settled back, struggling for control. Intense rage suddenly ravaged all the beauty from her face. He seemed to see her soul for the first time, with all its cold calculation, its avarice, its need to dominate. Then Lee Dagget spoke from the door.

"I told you he wouldn't go through with it, Kerry."

Hogarth wheeled to see the man standing in the open doorway. He had a six-shooter in one hand. The dust of the long ride was still caked like chalk on his haggard face, and the stink of his bearskin coat crept against Hogarth. He grinned balefully.

"I stopped to hide the horse and get a gun at the bunk shack," he said. "I thought you'd be back here to save Kerry." His eyes moved to the woman. Something salacious entered his grin. "It looks like you'll have to take me after all, Kerry."

She did not answer. Hogarth could hear her breathing softly behind him. Slowly the grin left Dagget's face. His eyes narrowed, giving his face a wolfish look.

"He knows it all," he said. Again Kerry did not answer. His voice grew thin. "You'd better make the choice."

"I think it's your choice," she said.

Hogarth saw the man moisten his lips, saw the gun move slightly in his hand, felt the prickling of tension run through his own body. Then the stutter of a horse on hard ground outside came to them. Dagget could not help his response. His head had turned, his body had started wheeling around before he could check himself. In that instant Hogarth lunged at the man, throwing himself in a dive at Dagget's knees. Dagget wheeled back, trying to fire. Hogarth's body struck his knees before Dagget could jerk the gun down into line, and it exploded while it was still aimed above Hogarth's body.

Dagget spilled backward, out onto the porch, with Hogarth sprawling across him. On his back beneath Hogarth, Dagget brought the gun around in a wild arc. It whipped across Hogarth's face, knocking him backward. As he pitched back, however, Hogarth lashed out blindly with a boot. He felt it

212

crack against Dagget's wrist, knocking the gun from his hand. The weapon hit with a thump and skittered across the porch. Thrown into a sitting position against the wall, half blinded by the blow from the gun, Hogarth threw himself flat onto his left side. This move left his right arm free to draw. He saw Dagget scoop up his six-shooter, saw him whirl back, still on his knees.

Hogarth's gun was in his fist, and his left hand was slapping across the hammer. The bullet knocked Dagget backward, causing him to lunge up to his feet with the force of the blow and the sudden shocking pain. His body struck the porch rail, and he flipped into the yard below.

Hogarth got to his feet, watching the dust settle back about the man's motionless body. The galloping horse came into the funnel of light spilling from the door now. Short-horse Simms dropped off a lathered animal and came running for the steps.

"You're all right?" he shouted. "I thought you. . . ?"

He stopped half way up the stairs. He was staring inside, a strange expression on his face. Squinting with the pain of Dagget's blow, Hogarth moved to the door. Kerry lay in the middle of the living room, a pitiful heap of dark green silk and pale flesh and rust-red hair. The bullet had hit her just beneath the left breast, and the front of her dress was soaked in blood. Dagget's bullet, going over Hogarth's lunging body, had driven into Kerry where she had stood behind Hogarth.

Hogarth was seized by grief and by a tremendous, devouring sense of irretrievable loss as he rushed to the body of the woman he had loved. He gathered her into his arms, and for the first time in many years he wept aloud, wept for Kerry, for Waco, for what they all had lost.

Shorthorse Simms turned from the door, went down the

steps, and hurried toward the bunkhouse where Joe Hide and the other hands were crowding out into the night, alarmed by the sound of the gunfire.

Chapter Twenty-One

There was an inquest the next day in the back of Ab Kidder's store. The position of the bodies, the number of bullets fired, and Simms's testimony exonerated Hogarth. As Hogarth and Simms left the store, they ran into a crowd gathered in the street outside. Lieutenant Bannister and his troop, half of them dismounted and bunched at the curb, had arrived in town. On the sidewalk Hogarth saw Wastewin and the old woman.

"We were coming back from the north," Bannister told Hogarth and Simms. "We found her singing at the Medicine Wheel. Some sort of dirge. She said Yellow Elk had died."

Bannister left to get his troop mounted, and Simms said he was going to have a drink at the Bullhorn. Hogarth was left alone with Wastewin and the old woman. Wastewin was worn and tired, and there was a resigned sadness in her face.

"They told me what happened with your woman," she said. "Will you leave the basin now?"

"Funny," he said. "Funny . . . to see the things you once thought meant so much in their true light. Maybe it takes something as violent as this to make you see them that way. I wonder if a man can change, after a lifetime of the things that formed him."

"There is nothing wrong with strength, or ambition, or expedience," she said. "Only in how you use them."

"When I saw you that time, Wastewin, up at Yellow Elk's camp, I had a feeling of being cleansed, of leaving all the hatred and the bitterness of the basin behind. I didn't understand it then."

She began breathing more deeply.

"Were you jealous of Kerry?"

Her lips grew full and heavy, but her eyes were sad. "Only of her freedom," she said simply.

He took her hand in his. A kind of glow came into her face, but it did not dispel the sadness. She did not speak, for she seemed to understand how it was inside him.

"Waco said there was a taint on this basin," he said then. "For the first time in my life I think he had the right idea, and I was wrong. He wanted to ride out." He stopped speaking, remembering the expression on Waco's face, as he held him with one arm, the smoking six-gun in the other.

Her hand tightened in his, and her eyes now were smoky.

"But you're still free, Hogarth, free to roam. The grass, and the sky, and the trees are yours."

The lieutenant rode up.

"I'm sorry, but you and your aunt will have to mount up now," he said to Wastewin.

Hogarth embraced her and then helped Wastewin's aunt to get mounted. As they rode out with the troopers, Hogarth stood in the center of the street, watching after them, the mountains forming icy silhouettes, aloof, silent, in the background. There was a vacant, empty look in his eyes. Then he turned, walked to the hitch rack, and mounted. He did not look back again as he rode slowly out of town, headed in the opposite direction, toward the Rocker T.

THE END

About the Author

Les Savage, Jr. was an extremely gifted writer who was born in Alhambra, California, but grew up in Los Angeles. His first published story was "Bullets and Bullwhips" accepted by the prestigious Street & Smith's *Western Story Magazine*. Almost ninety more magazine stories all set on the American frontier followed, many of them published in Fiction House magazines such as *Frontier Stories* and *Lariat Story Magazine* where Savage became a superstar with his name on many covers. His first novel, TREASURE OF THE BRASADA, appeared in 1947, the first of twenty-four published novels to appear in the next decade. Due to his preference for historical accuracy, Savage often ran into problems with book editors in the 1950s who were concerned about marriages between his protagonists and women of different races — a commonplace on the real frontier but not in much Western fiction in that decade. As a result of the censorship imposed on many of his works, only now have they been fully restored by returning to the author's original manuscripts. TABLE ROCK, published in 1993 in the United States by Walker and Company, in 1994 in the United Kingdom by Robert Hale, Ltd., and available in full-length audio from Books on Tape, was Savage's last book, initially suppressed by his agent in part because of its sympathetic depiction of Chinese on the frontier. More recently FIRE DANCE AT SPIDER ROCK (Five Star Westerns, 1995) and MEDICINE WHEEL (Five Star Westerns, 1996) have appeared.

Savage died young, at thirty-five, from complications arising out of hereditary diabetes and elevated cholesterol. However, his considerable legacy lives after him, there to reach a new generation of readers. His reputation as one of the finest authors of Western and frontier fiction continues and is winning new legions of admirers, both in the United States and abroad. Such noteworthy titles as SILVER STREET WOMAN, RETURN TO WARBOW, and BEYOND WIND RIVER have become classics of Western fiction. RETURN TO WARBOW is one of four of his novels so far to have appeared as a major motion picture. PHANTOMS IN THE NIGHT is the title of his next Five Star Western.

FIC SAVAGE ✓

Savage, Les.
Medicine wheel : a western
story.